Play Action Fake

Rangers Football
Book 1

Kameron Claire

Snuggle Whore Press, LLC

Copyright © 2023 by Kameron Claire

All rights reserved.

No part of this book may be reproduced in any form or by any electronic or mechanical means, including information storage and retrieval systems, without written permission from the author, except for the use of brief quotations in a book review.

This is a work of fiction. Names, characters, places, and incidents either are the products of the author's imagination or are used fictitiously based upon freely provided by fan submission. Any resemblance to actual persons, living or dead, businesses, companies, events, or locales is entirely coincidental.

Please respect the author and do not participate in or encourage piracy of copyrighted materials that would violate the author's rights.

Contains explicit love scenes and adult language. The suggested reading audience is 18 years or older.

Covers by SWP Covers

*To all the Witty, Wicked & Wild Readers...
Never let them silence our Witty tongues,
Never let them shame our Wicked needs,
Never let them stop our Wild deeds.*

Thank you for the love and support!

ROCKY MOUNTAIN
RANGERS

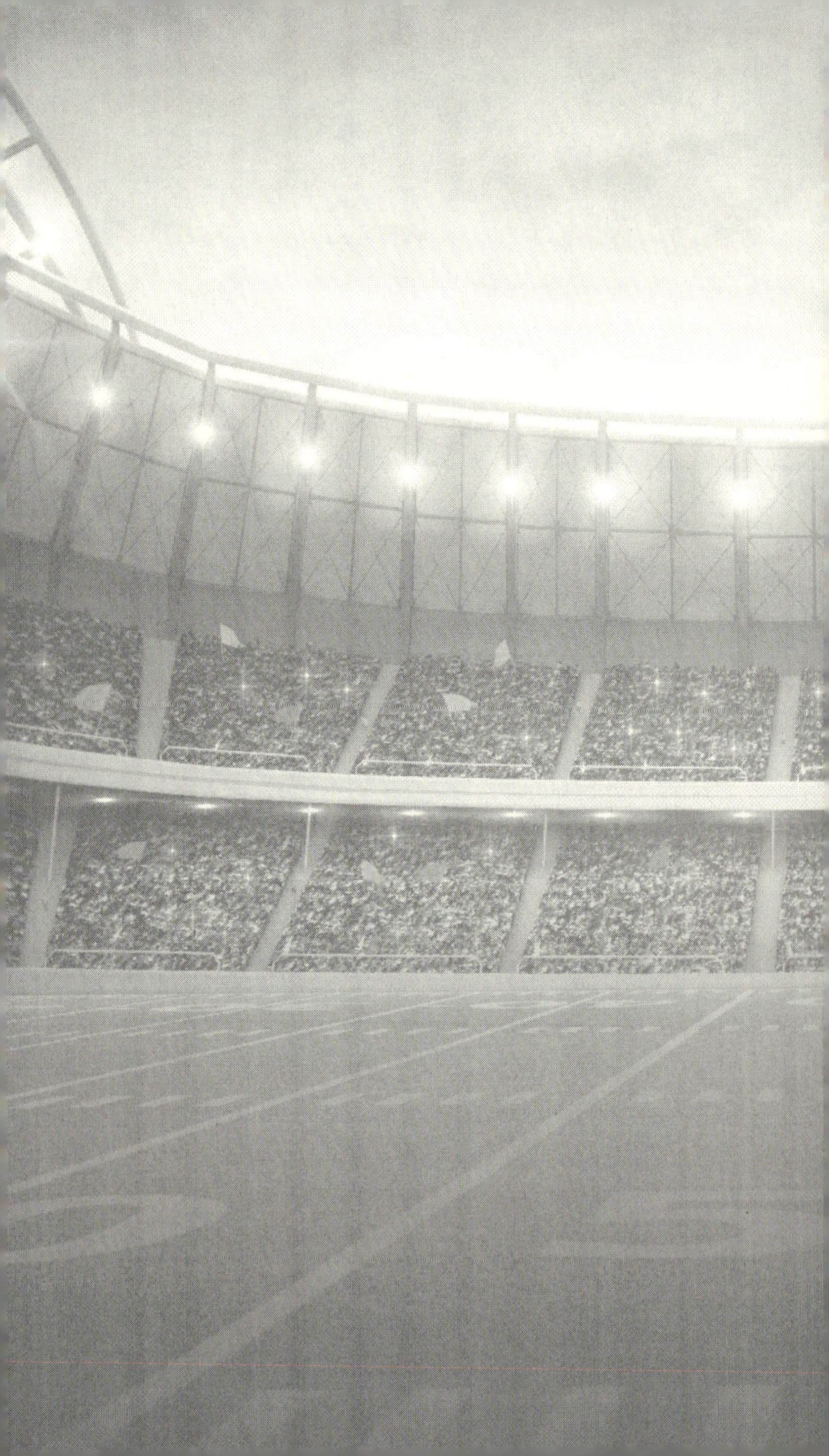

Prologue
Six years ago...

Scott drops back. He's looking for Taylor in the end zone. Pump action, Rylie Reynolds forces Scott out of the pocket. He scrambles to the left to avoid the sack, but Reynolds is on him, taking Scott down for a fifteen-yard loss.

That's a devastating sack for the Rangers on a must-score drive in the fourth quarter, Dan, but if there is a quarterback in the league who can recover from this, it's Deacon Scott.

It looks like there's a problem on the field, Mike.

Yeah, Deacon has yet to get up and the Rangers medical team is rushing the field.

Let's look at the playback.

It looks like a clean hit by Reynolds, but see how Deacon Scott's head and shoulders hit the ground here. I don't know, maybe this is precautionary measures as part of the concussion protocol?

Whatever it is, he appears to be conscious as he has

his eyes open. They're bringing out the stretcher and cart now. I have yet to see Deacon Scott lift his head or move his arms or legs, though.

If this proves to be a serious injury, this would be a catastrophic loss for the Rangers team at this point in the season.

Nine and three, and currently leading their division, the Rangers under the leadership of Deacon Scott have a real chance of a championship game this year, but I don't know the team has what they need in their backup quarterback Andrew Pearson to make it through the playoffs.

No player likes to see this, Dan. The stadium is quiet as the Ranger fans wait with bated breath for a sign that their beloved quarterback is okay.

Look at Reynolds, Mike. He seems very upset as he's pacing the field, trying to talk to Scott. There's a scuffle between players—tensions on the field are no doubt high facing the loss of their star quarterback.

Referees are giving the teams a five-minute break as the medical team clears the field. We'll let the people at home know more as they release information.

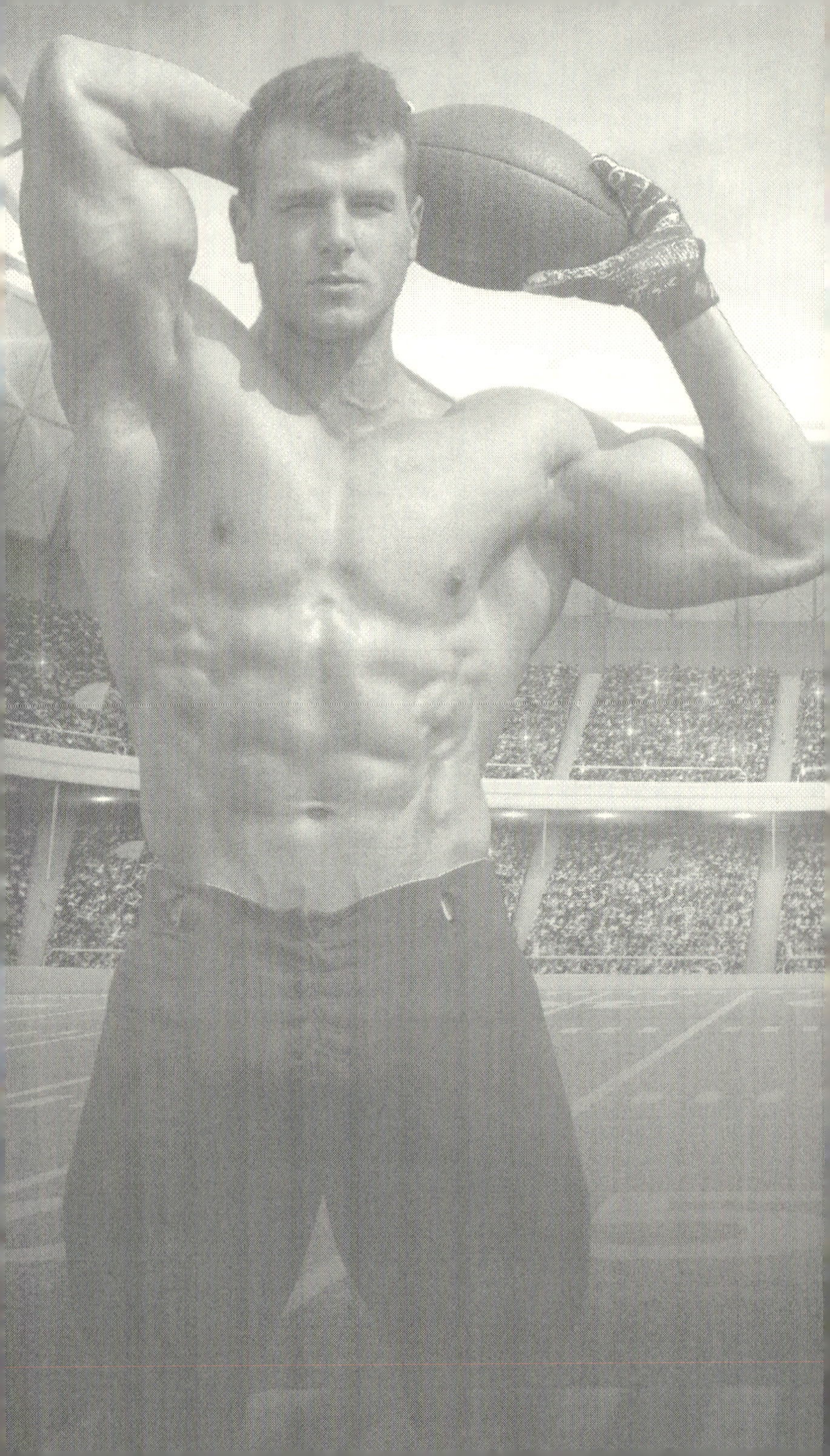

Chapter One
Deacon

"What are you saying?" I shove my fingers into my hair and pull, next-level frustration causing me to lose my cool.

My father sighs and leans back in his chair—a telltale sign for me to relax. "I'm saying, son, that as things stand right now, you can't be GM next year."

"Is this new?"

"Actually, it's always been in the bylaws. It was never a problem for me because I was married to your mother right after college."

Grumbling, I lean against the bookcase with my arms crossed over my chest. We are two weeks away from our first preseason game, and as the Director of Football Operations, I don't have time for this nonsense. "Remind me why they put such a ridiculous rule in the bylaws of this organization? What does being married have to do with running a goddamn football team?"

"Your great-grandfather's point was that this is a

family organization, and therefore, family needs to be running it."

I shake my head. "I am the next logical choice for GM. You've been grooming me for three years, and while I'm in no hurry to kick you out of the seat, there isn't anyone else in this organization better suited to replace you."

My father sighs. "Be that as it may—your grandfather has instructed me to bring Tyler and Timothy on to get them up to speed."

My arms flail as my temper rises. "Are you kidding me? Uncle Tyler played baseball in college and so did Tim. What do they know about running a professional football team?"

Shaking his head, my father pinches the bridge of his nose. "It doesn't matter. They understand professional sports, and more importantly, they are Scotts with families and a legacy to pass this team on to."

I slump into my chair. "This is so unfair. I've dedicated my life to football, gave my body to this team and almost my life. When would I have had time to find a girlfriend, much less a wife?"

"I understand, son. Simple fact is this football team has been owned and operated by the Scotts for three generations, and your great-grandfather wants to ensure it continues on for another three generations. He's the one who wrote this into the bylaws back in 1966 when he enfranchised the team. My father is only enforcing his wishes."

"This is such bullshit." My mind spins with ways out of this, but I'm coming up with nothing.

Daniel Declan Scott III—he saved me and my brother from being a fourth, thank god—watches me closely and waves his hand in the air, as if performing a magic trick. "If you were serious with someone, I might get your grandfather to be flexible for a bit, but the fact is I need to spend this season grooming the next GM so your grandfather can retire at the end of the season—and because of your bachelor status, you are not it."

And then an idea hits me.

A crazy, brilliant, probably horrible idea. "What if I was dating someone?"

"Seriously dating?"

I shrug. "Fairly serious."

My father's brow furrows. "Who? Who are you seriously dating that none of us have heard about before?"

I glance at the stack of unanswered mail on my desk, my fifteen-year high school reunion invitation sitting on top. When I talked to the organizer a couple months ago, I told her I'd be too busy to attend a reunion in August, but where else can I meet a couple dozen single women who basically know who I am in one night? "A woman I knew in high school. She's on the reunion committee and hit me up a few months ago. We've been dating ever since."

My father narrows his eyes and purses his lips. He doesn't believe a word coming out of my mouth and we both know it. "A woman from high school?"

My father and I know each other very well, so I'm not

going to try to bullshit him. "Do you think Granddad will cut me some slack if I had a serious girlfriend?"

"If you were really serious, you'd make her your fiancée." His brow raises in challenge.

I nod. "I can do that."

He stands and raps his knuckles against my desk before spinning on his heels to walk out. "I can put your grandfather off for another week or two, but after that, you're going to be seeing a lot more of your uncle Tyler, so you better produce this fiancée in a hurry."

I walk into the ballroom of the Overlook Hotel, a dozen or more sets of eyes tracking my every movement and murmuring to each other, "*Oh my God, that's Deacon Scott.*"

Son of a bitch.

I can't believe I'm at my high school reunion. I barely remember attending this school. When I stepped onto the practice field my freshman year, I already had my sights set on college.

This is fucking crazy.

"Deacon?"

A black-haired beauty with dark red lips and kohl-rimmed eyes stares at me, but there's nothing warm or inviting about the scowl on her face. She sits at the registration table, and I wonder if this is the London I flirted with on the phone for a whole three minutes a couple of months ago.

"Present and accounted for." I throw her my patented charm-the-pants-off-the-press smile.

Her eyes narrow, clearly unimpressed. "You said you weren't coming."

"I changed my mind. Why? Is it going to be a problem? It's not like there's plated meals or something you had to have a headcount for."

She closes her eyes, and I swear I can hear her counting to three, praying to the gods for patience. I've seen my mother do this, but never a femme fatale near my age with painted, kissable, pouty lips. "No, but, if the most successful person from Pinehurst High had RSVP'd, we would've gotten more attendees to come to a fifteen-year reunion."

I place my hand on the table and lean forward, as if to tell her a secret between the two of us. "Did you ever think maybe that's the reason I didn't RSVP?"

The scowl on her face fades, and she stares up at me with something akin to appreciation. "Good point. I guess if I were you, I wouldn't want anybody knowing where I was going to be, either."

Maybe it's the black-on-black-on-black ensemble, but her eyes are a mesmerizing purple-gray, and I'd love to see what color they are in the sunlight. I bet they sparkle like diamonds in the midnight sky. "Thank you for understanding. I assume you're London?"

"All day, every day."

"It's nice to meet you. I'm sorry if this comes off as rude, but I don't remember you." She's got a look that says *don't look at me, don't fuck with me, don't even think about me*, and yet I see the bombshell underneath. She has a silky smooth complexion and is fair enough that I bet she turns bright red when she blushes, or better yet, when she comes.

Fuck me, I've never been turned on by a goth chick before, but maybe that's because I've never taken the time to look past the surface. I feel like I would have noticed London even back then.

She snorts. "That's because I wasn't part of the cool kid club."

My brows shoot up, and I snap my head back like someone has slapped me. "There was a cool kid club?"

Rolling her eyes, she folds her arms over her chest, which only hoists up the breasts covered by a high, silken Victorian-style collar. "Only a member of the cool kids' club would say that."

"Sorry, but I don't remember joining."

"That's because you didn't have to join. You created it by being born." She drops her arms as if she realizes how bitchy she's coming off. "Still, I'm not surprised you don't remember me, even though I interviewed you for the yearbook and the school blog."

My jaw drops. I remember her. Not her name, but that interview. "That was you?"

"You remember that?"

"Yeah, I do. You were the first female I'd met outside of my family who actually asked insightful questions about being a football player versus what car I was going to buy when I went pro or—" I bat my eyelashes dramatically "—do I date cheerleaders?"

London smiles, her dark painted lips separating to flash straight white teeth with a small chip in the front. "You're funny."

I shrug. "I have my days."

She glances at the people milling around in the room behind me and then brings her intriguing eyes back to me. "Well, Mr. Scott, I don't think you need a name tag as it looks like all of your groupies are champing at the bit to say hello."

I glance over my shoulder at the crowd and sigh. "Aren't you coming inside to socialize?"

"Hell no. Why else would I have volunteered to run the registration desk? This gives me five seconds of interaction, and then I send people on their way to *people*."

"We've been talking for over five seconds—does that make me special?"

She narrows her eyes and bites her lip to suppress a smile. "I don't think you need me to stroke your ego."

Damn, I like this girl. She's got a no-bullshit approach to life. She's not trying to impress me, and she's not impressed by me either, which only makes me want to get to know her.

Dammit, Deacon! You're not here to find a girlfriend.

You're here to find a fiancée—or at least a girl/friend who will pretend to be your fiancée—preferably one you won't fall for. This is a business arrangement, not a love connection.

"How much longer until you roll up the welcome mat?" I grab a name tag and write on it, if for no other reason than to drag out my time with her.

She glances at her phone. "The event started ten minutes ago, so I'll give it another twenty before I close up shop. You know, for those of you that like to be fashionably late."

Is it weird that I love how she gives me shit?

"Have a drink with me before you go."

Her furrowed brow answers me with a resounding no. "Why?"

"I find you interesting." I glance over my shoulder purposefully. "And something tells me you'll be the only one providing me with stimulating conversation tonight."

She laughs, an honest-to-goodness laugh that sounds like soothing church bells far in the distance. "Fine. One drink."

"I'll wait for you at the bar." I peel the sticker and slap the name tag on my chest. On it, I wrote, *Cool Kid*. London eyes the name tag and laughs again. "Don't make me come looking for you. See you in twenty."

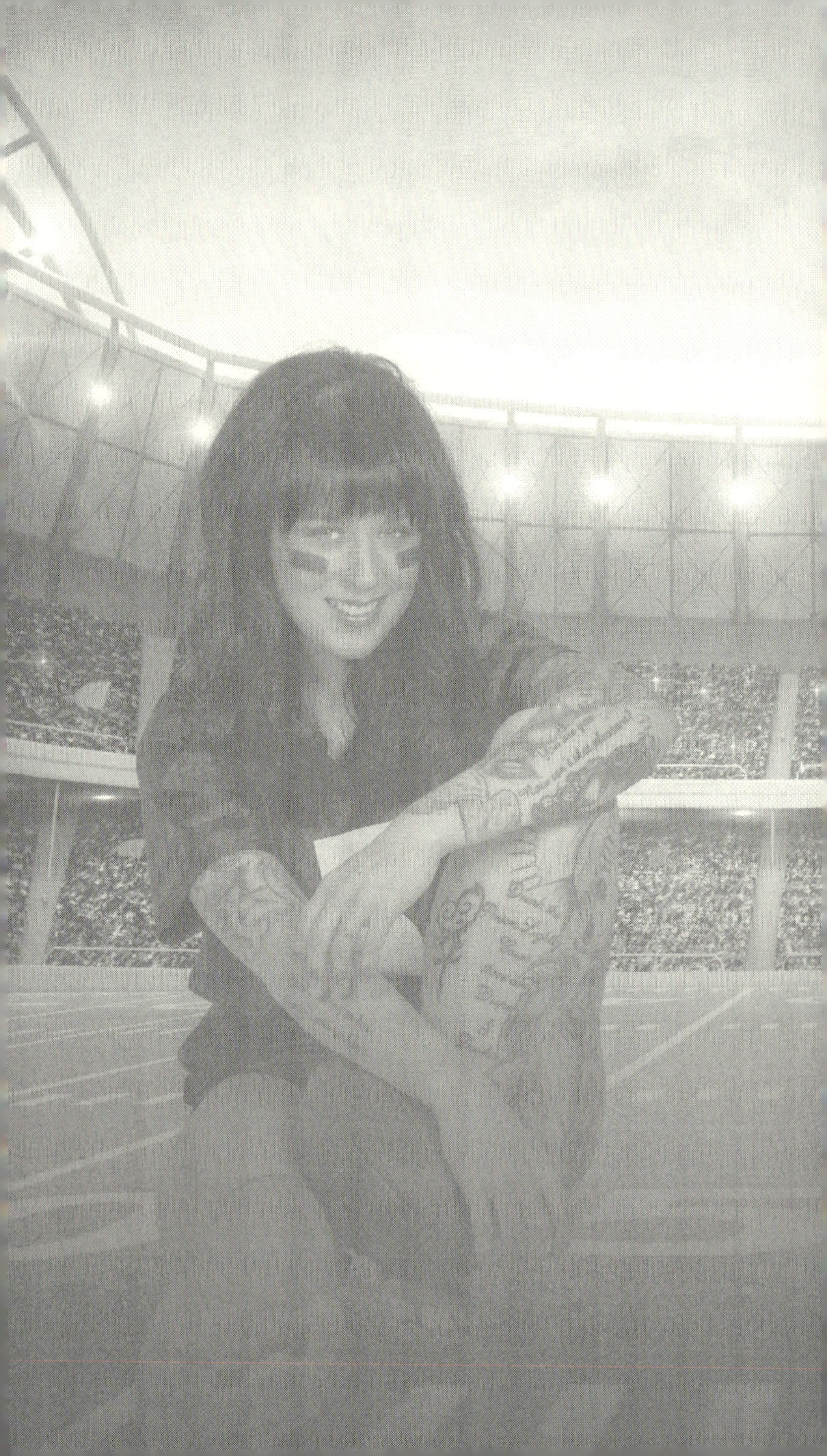

Chapter Two
London

Why do I get the impression that Deacon *fucking* Scott is flirting with me?

The fact I'm associated with my high school reunion —much less volunteering for it, considering how detrimental my high school years were to my psyche—is astonishing. This is definitely another topic for my bi-weekly therapy sessions where I rant and rave, but never actually resolve any of my trauma.

I watch the larger-than-life man walk away, and he's even more drool-worthy than he was in high school. Back then, he was a beautiful teenage boy. Tall and muscled, he carried himself with a confident swagger that the rest of the guys on his football team only faked. He was never mean, never a bully, but so focused on his future that I think he was only going through the motions of high school to prepare for what lie ahead. If I remember correctly—and I don't know why I wouldn't since I practically have a degree in all things Deacon Scott—he always had a date to every high school milestone. Homecoming, winter formal, and prom. But even though he always had someone on his arm, I don't remember him dating someone.

Not seriously, anyway.

Now, well—he's who he was then, but tenfold. Taller, more muscled, more chiseled, and even more droolworthy. But he's also got a raw edge to his formerly all-American clean-cut image, and a vibe that says I'm a nice guy, but I really like getting dirty between the sheets.

Or maybe I'm projecting my own desires onto him.

He wasn't wrong when he said I asked him insightful questions during our interview. I know football. It was the only thing that connected my dad and me when I was a kid. I was the son my father never had, yelling at the TV every Sunday from ten a.m. until bedtime. I followed Deacon Scott's illustrious career after high school. An All-Pro quarterback, he won the Heisman Trophy his senior year at Clemson University, and then came home to play for the Rocky Mountain Rangers—the team his grandfather owns. While the home team has always done okay—rarely at the top, but never at the bottom of their division—they flourished under Deacon as quarterback, winning their first divisional championship in over forty years.

I still vividly recall the career-ending sack against the Denver Mustangs, where Rylie Reynolds took Deacon to the ground in a brutal blitz that crushed three vertebrae in his upper back. The horror of watching the screen as the medical team swarmed Deacon, the crowd watching anxiously as the camera tried to get up-close images of him, and the sorrow the whole stadium felt as he was carted off the field, motionless and strapped to a gurney—I remember it like it was yesterday.

There was a time the news outlets warned he may never walk again, but I knew better. I remembered the determined high schooler who'd had one goal and achieved it. So, I knew he'd not only walk, but play again, if he wanted to.

He came back for one game—just to prove he could—but with his little brother coming up in the ranks, he graciously handed the team over to Declan Scott and took a management position within the organization.

After that, cyberstalking Deacon became harder with little-to-no press being printed about him. I have no idea what he's been up to for the last three years.

What I do know is he's still rich, still hot, and still one of the most eligible bachelors in Spring City.

Why the fuck does he want to get a drink with me?

I watch as the sheep flock to him. Bleach blonde Barbies with their fake smiles and even faker tits. They're all former members of the cool kids' club but were mean and territorial about their circle, bullying anyone they set their sights on. One day, in the middle of our sophomore year, I became their target. They tortured me for the next two and a half years of my high school existence.

It's a miracle I survived.

A couple more people walk off the elevator with nowhere to go but the ballroom. I recognize most of them, even though I don't engage, and check them against the registration. I hand them name tags and markers, and thank the gods they don't recognize me—or if they do, don't pay me any attention.

When they asked me to be on the reunion committee, it was because of my graphic design skills I'd used as part of the yearbook and blog. Also, Maryanne Merryweather —the corniest name they could bless a girl our age with— is on the committee, and she's one of my only friends. When she asked, I couldn't say no.

Maryanne stands in the ballroom's doorway and smiles at the people walking in, but her eyes keep coming back to me. I know she saw Deacon talking to me and now wants to gossip. As soon as my table is clear, she comes dancing over on her tiptoes. "Oh my God! Deacon Scott came after all. I thought you said he declined."

"He did."

"What did he say?"

I shrug. "He wants to have a drink."

"WHAT?!?!" Maryanne loses all semblance of cool.

"Shhh!" I snatch her hand and pull her close. "Are you kidding me right now?"

"Sorry." She bites her lip. "But that is major news."

"It's nothing. He's probably baiting me so the rest of the goon squad can tease me about one of a hundred things."

"No. He wasn't like that." Maryanne is the sweetest person I know. She's got a good heart and only sees the best in people. Somehow, she toed the line between the cool kids and the losers in high school, never actually accepted as one of them, but never bullied either. She lives in the interim, where she blissfully ignores the nastiness in this world.

Not that she's naïve.

She's very aware of the ugliness in people's hearts, but somehow, she looks past it. I honestly don't know how she does it. She's the Top 40s in my otherwise classic Emo world, but I love her for it.

"I know, but why else would he want to have a drink?"

"Maybe he wants to confess a fifteen-year-long crush?"

I narrow my eyes and purse my lips. "He didn't remember me."

"Oh, well, that would make a lifelong crush difficult."

Snorting, I roll my eyes. "You think?"

"So, what are you going to do?" Maryanne sits her plump butt on the edge of my table, her soft lavender top and long flowing skirt riddled with flowers giving her a pastel hue akin to her sweet approachable personality. Couple her outfit with her auburn hair that is perpetually pulled back from her face and cherub cheeks, she looks like a soccer mom armed with snack packs versus a vibrant single woman co-chairing a successful charitable organization.

"In fifteen minutes, I'm grabbing my bag and sneaking out of here."

"No! You can't do that." Maryanne grabs my hand and pulls it to her chest. "You have to at least hear what he has to say."

"Ugh, Maryanne. My therapy bills are high enough. I

can't afford weekly visits nor medication. Subjecting myself to potential embarrassment is more than my bank account can manage."

"Please, for me, be an optimist this one time and hope for the best."

I roll my eyes again, but I can't resist my little care bear. "Okay. I'll give him five minutes and then I'm out of here."

Deacon is standing at the bar as he promised with a swarm of people milling around him. I refuse to enter the lion's den, but I don't have to because as soon as I enter the ballroom, his attention snaps to me. He watches as I cross the room and take up space at the end of the bar, a sly smile spreading his perfect lips.

And then, to my utter shock, he excuses himself from the group and joins me. "What are you having?"

"Uh, Shirley Temple, extra temple." I say to the bartender who furrows his brow. Clarifying, I add, "extra grenadine."

"Gotcha. And for you?" he says to Deacon, who holds up a scotch on the rocks or something similar.

"I'm covered." Deacon smiles at me. "No alcohol?"

"Not tonight." I'm not going to tell him I never drink. Alcoholism runs in my family, my father spending most of my life in a bottle. He's not a mean drunk—so you don't have to feel sorry for me—but a fully functioning alcoholic who has a hard time holding down a job and looks at least twenty years older than he is. I love my dad, but I don't always like him, especially since he refuses to acknowledge his problem.

"So, what have you been up to for the last fifteen years?" Deacon says after the bartender puts down my fancy cherry 7-Up.

"Really? You care about what I've been doing?" I play with my straw, attempting to stab the cherry in the glass's bottom.

He frowns for the first time, and I have to say, I'm sorry to do that to him. He's too beautiful to frown. "You seem to have a chip on your shoulder. Did I do something to you in high school?"

"You? No." I glance over his shoulder at the crowd staring at us. "Your peers were less than hospitable."

"I'm sorry to hear that. I honestly don't remember much from back then."

I relax a little and let him off the hook. He's absolutely right, and I have no reason to punish him for the actions of others. "You wouldn't. You had your future laid out in front of you and were very driven as a teenager."

"I'm still very driven." He pauses and then takes a sip of his drink. "So, are you going to tell me what you've been up to?"

I shrug. "Nothing really. I went to massage therapy school instead of college, do a bit of freelance graphic design work when I can, and live in a one-bedroom apartment with a black and white tuxedo cat named Crow."

"No husbands, boyfriends—" he smiles and quickly adds "—girlfriends?"

"Maybe a couple over the years." I refuse to clarify further.

His smile grows wider.

"And how about you?"

He takes another sip of his drink. "What do you want to know that you don't already know?"

"What makes you think I know stuff?"

"Well, if I remember correctly from our one interaction, you are a football fan and, therefore, are probably aware of my career highlights."

I blush and duck my head. "Yeah, I know about them. I'm glad you recovered from that nasty sack. You scared a lot of people that day."

"I pissed off a lot of gamblers, too. Apparently my almost being paralyzed lost a lot of people money." He shakes his head.

"Rumor is the team signed Rylie Reynolds this year. How weird is that?"

Deacon shrugs. "I'm the one who recruited him. It was a clean hit, and mentally, I think the injury affected him more than it did me. He's a fantastic defensive back and we need him on our side."

"That's very mature of you."

"Don't tell anyone." He winks.

"London bridges going down!" Joe Hyland, former offensive lineman, now number one loser, sidles up to us. The crowd behind him chuckles as my cheeks grow hot. It's obvious he's drunk by the volume of his voice and the way he staggers. "How you doing, girl? Still got those knee pads?"

I sigh and grab my purse, turning on my heels before he can say another word. "It was nice talking to you, Deacon."

I'm in the parking lot, digging my keys to my dilapidated car out of my purse, when I hear heavy footsteps approach. I spin around, prepared to gouge Joe in the throat with my self-defense keychain, when Deacon raises his hand in surrender. "Hey, hey. Where are you going?"

"I'm going home."

"Why? I mean, yeah, I get why you'd want to leave here, but do you have to go home? Let's find another place and have a drink."

I cross my arms over my chest. "Look. I don't know what game you are playing, Deacon Scott, but whatever you think you know about me, it isn't true. It wasn't true in high school, and it sure the fuck isn't true now."

"Look, London, I've been around locker room trash talk my whole life, and I know bullshit when I hear it. I don't know which rumor Joe was trying to rekindle, and I don't care to know. I spent less than thirty minutes inside that ballroom, and the ten minutes I spent talking to you were the highlight." He shoves his hands in his pockets. "And, to be honest, the last time I remotely flirted with a woman was when I talked to you four months ago. So, give me a break, yeah? I just want to get to know you."

I sigh and check my phone for the time. Maryanne would kill me if I didn't give him half a shot. "There's a coffee and gelato shop two blocks from here. Want a scoop?"

"Gelato? Hell yeah. I love ice cream." He grins and I'm reminded of the nice guy from high school. The one that smiled and said hello to random strangers—me being one of those strangers from time to time.

I can't help it. Looking at his handsome face with hazel-green eyes, I melt a little.

Deacon Scott is worming his way into my frosty heart.

Shit.

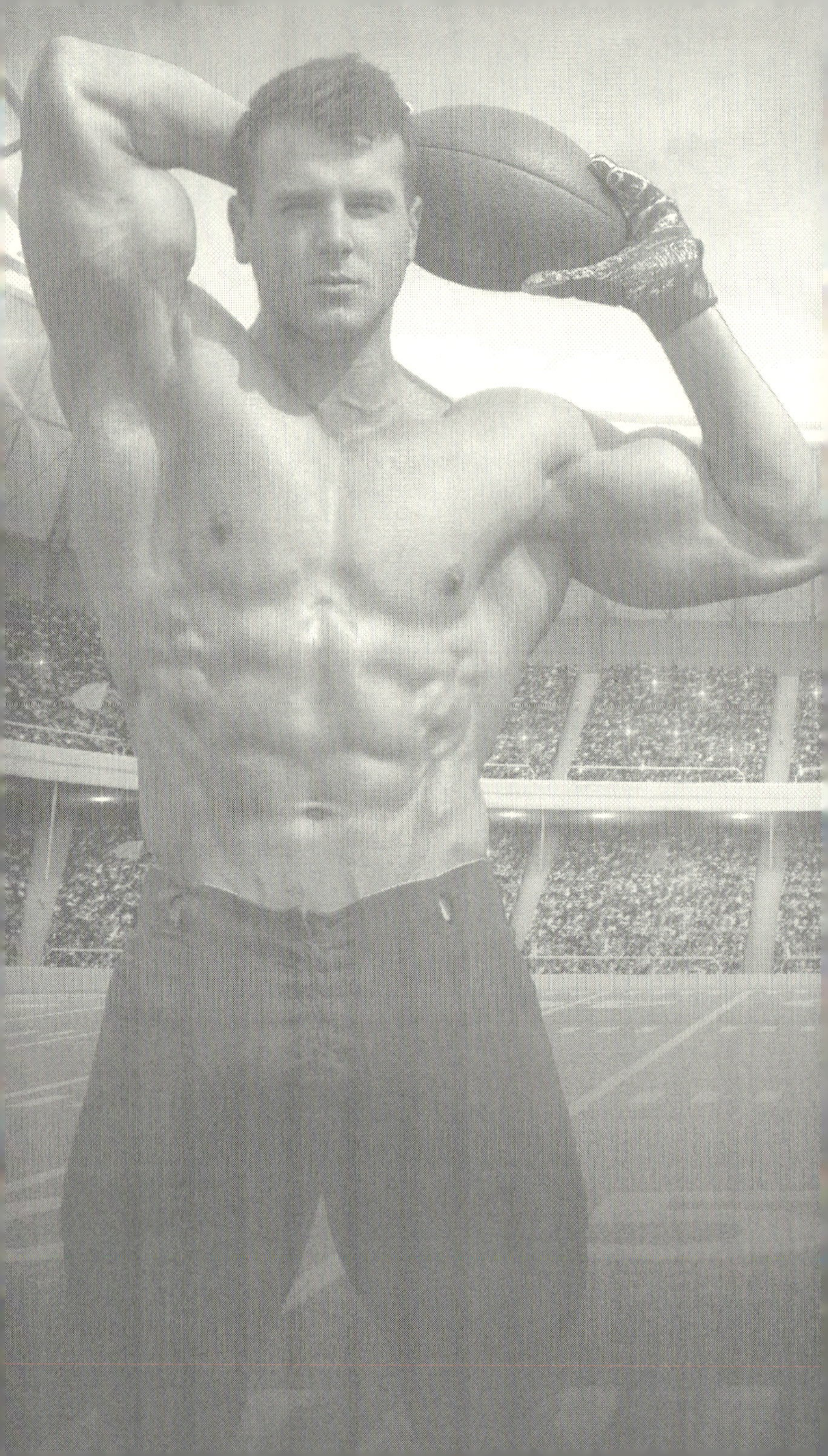

Chapter Three
Deacon

When London's car won't start, we walk the two blocks to the cafe. The place is hopping for eight o'clock, but we find a table outside to sit with our coffee and gelato.

I lied back there in the parking lot. I do know which rumor Joe Hyland was referring to because I made him tell me before I hauled ass out of the ballroom. The sheer lunacy of the story tells me it's not true, but every ridiculous story almost always has a sliver of truth to it.

Drunk at a party our sophomore year, a few football players lined up to feed her their dicks while she knelt on a pair of shin guards, taking cum shot after cum shot to the face.

It's a ludicrous story, and something only awful high schoolers would start. No wonder she wants nothing to do with our classmates. It makes me wonder why she would take part in the planning at all?

"Does your car not start often?" I ask over a spoonful of hazelnut.

"More often than I would like." She shrugs.

"Why don't you buy a new one?"

Her eyebrow quirks, and she shakes her head. "Not everyone can afford to buy a car whenever theirs runs out of gas."

A slight blush hits my cheeks. She called me out on my privilege, and she's absolutely right. "I'm sorry. I didn't mean it like that. It's just, having reliable transportation is so important, especially in this town, considering our mass transit is abysmal and they spread everything out."

"I'm sorry, too." She dips her head. "My go-to personality trait is defensive, and I shouldn't have snapped at you. Money is tight right now and keeping a roof over my head is my number one priority."

"What do you do for money?"

Her eyes narrow, but she catches herself, her facial features relaxing. "As I said before, I'm a massage therapist when I can get clients. And I freelance graphic design work—again, when I can get clients."

"What do you mean, when you can get clients?"

"Well, I'm not working out of a spa right now, and I don't have my own office to massage at, so I limit my client list to those who want in-home therapy. You can imagine the creeps who try to get a single female to come to their home to *massage* them, so that makes my client list tiny."

Warring heat rushes through my veins.

One, I can imagine having her massage me, and it's hot.

Two, I want to pummel anyone who would try to take advantage of her. She's got this tough girl vibe, and yet, I have an insane desire to protect and shield her from everything that turned her into this jaded, tarnished black pretty package.

"What kind of massage do you do?"

"Not that kind."

I chuckle, desperate to break through her shell. "Seriously. Sports medicine? Deep tissue?"

She nods. "And trigger point. Originally, I wanted to get into physical therapy and rehabilitation, so I perused a few certifications."

"Do you want a job with the Rangers?"

We stare at each other for a full minute before she breaks out in laughter. "You're funny."

"I'm serious. I'll introduce you to the medical director for an interview."

"Why would you do that?"

"I like you, and you need a steady income. Plus, I guarantee you not one Ranger will ask you for a happy ending. Otherwise, I will end them."

She bites her lips, a pretty blush hitting her cheeks.

Dear God, my heart! She likes the idea of being protected. I can get on board with this.

"Would you grab dinner with me tomorrow night?" I pick up her empty ice cream cup and stack it with mine.

"Dinner?" She shakes her head. "I don't know—"

"What don't you know? Are you hesitant because we

went to high school together and your memories of that time and place suck?"

"Yes, that. Plus, you're Deacon Scott. You could have dinner with anyone."

"And yet the woman I'm asking to dinner is telling me no." I raise my eyebrow, which makes her smile.

"Okay. Dinner. Tomorrow night. Where?"

"I think I should pick you up, considering your car is unreliable. Speaking of which, let me call my guy and have him tow your car to the garage tonight so they can work on it tomorrow."

"I can't afford that right now, Deacon."

"My treat." I pull my phone out and text the family assistant, Phil, who takes care of my life better than I do.

"Wait. I don't know how long it will take to pay you back." She places her hand on mine to stop my texting action—her blue-black fingernails manicured and cut to the perfect length for a massage therapist—but I will not be dissuaded.

I won't trap her—my offer to help her with her car and get her an interview with the Rangers is legit—but I also need a fiancée soon, and I'm thinking she's perfect for the job. She knows how to play a role, as I suspect she has played a version of herself every day for most of her life, shielding her heart from those who might hurt her. She's got common sense and won't get all doe-eyed on me as we play through this charade. I could create a straightforward business arrangement between us, but I feel like this will go better and be more enjoyable for both of us if we can establish a friendship.

Hence dinner tomorrow night.

Phil responds with a thumbs up, and *Troy's Towing will be there in fifteen minutes.*

I smile at London. "It's already done. The tow company will meet us at your car in a few minutes. Let's head back."

———

An hour later, after following her car to the garage—because London needed control over where her vehicle sat overnight—I'm pulling up to her apartment on a not-great side of town. I wouldn't leave my car parked on the street, much less feel comfortable closing my eyes at night in this building, and I'm six-four, two hundred and twenty-five pounds. I'm assuming London is maybe five-six and one hundred and fifty pounds, not that I would ever ask her weight.

I'm not stupid.

I put my Lamborghini in park. While I have multiple cars, I went for ostentatious tonight, but now I regret it. Something tells me the Italian performance doesn't impress London.

"Should I walk you to your door?"

She smiles, but it's a half-flirtatious, half-taunting curve of her lips, and I know she's about to make fun of me. "Are you afraid of my hood?"

I glance at the three guys on the corner who eye my car with the same lust they might eye a naked woman. "I'll admit, it doesn't have the safest vibe."

She follows my gaze. "Those guys? That's David, Jo-Joe, and Playboy Bill. Funny enough, they keep me safe. They are going to freak when I get out of this car."

"Yeah, I guess we stand out. I'll pick you up in the Range Rover tomorrow night."

Laughing, she unbuckles her belt. "Yeah, because then you'll blend."

"Can I get your phone number?" I wave my phone in the air, fingers at the ready.

"Sure." She rattles off her digits and then pops open her door, the interior light coming on. The guys exclaim loud enough for the entire neighborhood to hear, "Holy shit, that's London!"

"With Deacon Scott!"

"Who?"

"All-Pro quarterback, Heisman Trophy winner, heir to the Rocky Mountain Rangers, Deacon Scott. The guy is worth like a bazillion dollars!"

"What's London doing with him?"

"Yo, London!"

She steps out of the car, but pops her head back in. "Did you get all that?"

I chuckle. "It was hard to miss. Should I introduce myself?"

"That would make their month."

I climb out of my car, my eyes on the trio who, now that I take a better look at them, have boyish faces despite their hardened shells. I really need to look past the surface when summing people up from afar. "Hey guys."

"Ah man!" The three come running and I realize they

are teenagers, maybe sixteen years old. We shake hands as they field a million questions so fast, they put a postgame press junket to shame.

"Whoa, guys. I didn't get one question."

London walks up behind them, slapping her palms on two of their shoulders. "Guys, chill out. He's just a normal man."

"Normal?" I grin at her. "And here I was going for extraordinary."

"I've already told you, if you want your ego stroked, I'm not your girl."

"You know him, London?" one kid asks. I still have no idea who is who, although I'm guessing the kid with Jo-Joe tattooed on his neck is, in fact, Jo-Joe.

At least I hope so.

"London and I went to high school together a million years ago," I add.

"You never told us that." The tallest kid with slicked back hair tosses her an accusatory look.

"We weren't friends in high school, PB." London shrugs.

"Are you now?" the heavy set kid asks, and I'm guessing this is David.

I quirk my brow and toss her an expectant look. She started this, so she can answer them—and me—at the same time.

"Maybe." She eyes me playfully.

"Man, you gotta be friends with Deacon Scott, London."

"Why do I have to?"

"Because he's cool," Jo-Joe says.

"He's famous," David adds.

"He's rich," PB finishes.

"Guys, I'm standing right here," I joke. "How about nice, funny, charming, and handsome?"

All three boys look me up and down. "Yeah, maybe, but being rich and famous is so much better."

"And there you go." London pats my arm, her fingers lingering on my bicep.

Hmmm. Wouldn't mind her doing that a bit more, exploring my body, letting me explore hers.

Shit. Gotta keep this business or else we're bound to fail.

Eye on the prize, Deacon.

The GM position.

"Can you guys make sure London gets to her apartment safely? She won't let me escort her to her door."

"Yeah, man. No problem."

I smile, clasping hands with each guy one more time. "All right. I'll see you guys around, and I'll see you later, London."

She gives me a nod. "Have a good night, Deacon."

Something tells me I can learn a lot from London—a fresh perspective on the world around us. I've always tried to be friendly and empathetic to strangers, but a touch of wariness lives deep within. I know I was born into privilege—my great-grandfather owned and sold large lots of land south of Spring City long before anyone thought to live here.

He was a rich man.

Play Action Fake

My grandfather is even richer.

Being an athlete has introduced me to people from all walks of life, football being their only shot at something better. I feel like I have a diverse group of friends because of my teammates, but my knee-jerk reaction to three boys, who most likely have been forced into being men long before their time, tells me I need to step out of my ivory tower for a tour and walk amongst my fans.

Meeting these three, who were genuinely excited to meet me, fills me with an energy akin to taking the field. I miss those days of running out of the tunnel to the deafening roar of thirty thousand fans.

Maybe I'll bring these guys Rangers gear tomorrow.

Maybe, eventually, box seats to a home game of their choice.

Either way, I'm excited about my impending friendship with London.

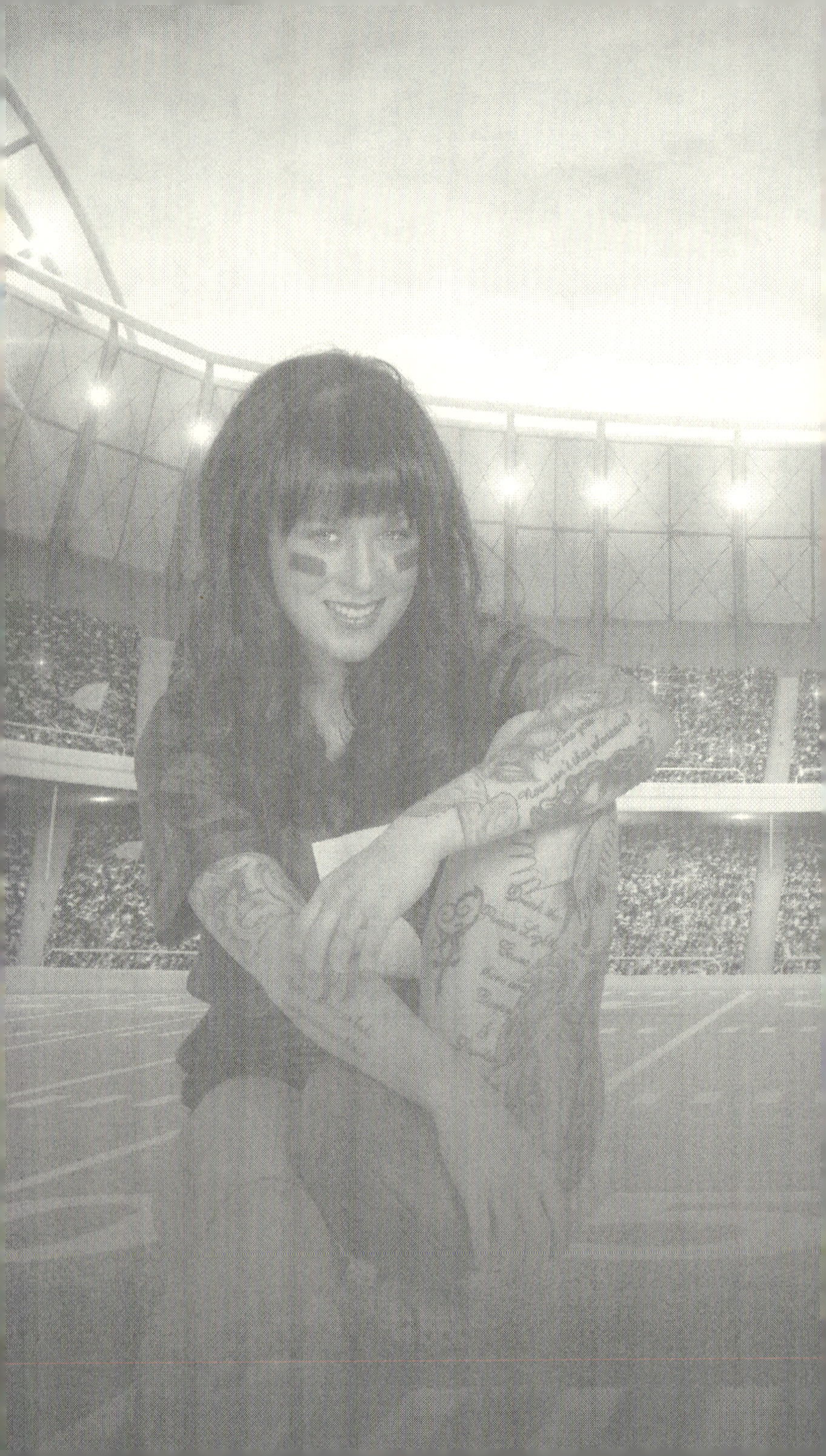

Chapter Four
London

"What happened to you last night? I heard laughter and saw you running out of there, but before I could break free, I saw Deacon running after you." Maryanne's voice comes through my speaker as I design a promotional package for her charity holiday fundraiser. If she didn't hire me on a recurring basis, I wouldn't eat.

"Oh, Joe Hyland tried to replay one of my greatest hits, much to my embarrassment."

"And?"

I smile. "Deacon and I went out for gelato. He drove me home, and we're going out tonight."

"Shut up!" Maryanne squeals, and then murmurs sorry—probably to the people in her office.

"It's nothing, I'm sure." I try to sound dismissive, but mostly I'm suspicious. I can't for the life of me understand why he wants to take me out, get to know me, fix my car—any of it. But I have nothing, so what do I have to lose?

"It's something. He could ask anyone out, but he wants you. What are you going to wear?"

"He said to keep it casual." I shrug, hoping my interpretation of casual and his are the same. Since we're having dinner and not going to a club, I've toned down the goth look. It's rare I take the time to don heavy eyeliner and deep red lipstick, anyway. Most of the time, I wear mascara and have my black hair pulled back into a simple ponytail. For dinner tonight, I'm wearing a black see-through blouse over a black tank top and jeans with ballet flats on my feet. I have my hair pulled back in combs, and I have the bare minimum makeup on, my lips tinted dark red with a shiny gloss over the top.

Unlike last night when I'd covered my arms and chest with a Victorian silk blouse, tonight my tattoos are on full display, and I'm curious how Deacon will respond to them. He said he wanted to get to know me because I'm interesting—how interesting, I don't think he knows—so I think it is best to give him me in totality on day one and let him run away screaming on the first night.

"Casual, but sexy. Right?" Maryanne teases.

"He didn't specify sexy, but like yours, my boobs have a mind of their own."

"Yeah, I love that about our bodies," she says dreamily. "Shoot, I've got to go. Call me tonight, or tomorrow if the night goes well."

I roll my eyes. "Later skater."

Play Action Fake

I glance at my text messages again, noting the hour. Deacon texted me around one—a totally respectable hour in the day. No cheesy early morning, *Hey Sexy* or *How'd you sleep?*

But a simple, *"Are we still on for six? I'm feeling Italian. How's that sit with you?"*

One, I like he isn't trying to make it feel like a date, even though—I mean technically—this is a date. Two, instead of asking me what I want, he takes charge. Like most women, I love a confident man who can make a decision. I have enough on my plate and appreciate the decisiveness followed by a check-in. If I was vehemently against Italian, I'd respond as such, but at least I know our starting point and we don't have to do the awkward—*what do you want? I don't know, whatever you want*—dance people do.

It's five minutes to six when I exit my apartment building to find Deacon standing outside of a lifted Jeep Wrangler with Jo-Joe, David, and Playboy Bill. Those guys rambled on to me for twenty minutes after he left last night, proving to me they're real Ranger fans. Playboy has a Rangers jersey on and Deacon is signing his chest.

"What is all of this?" I laugh at the guys who are just as much boys as they are men. Unfortunately, they have to grow up quick around here—their parents working full-time jobs, sometimes two—but I love them for it.

"Deacon brought us jerseys, London!"

"That was nice of you." I smile up at him.

He shrugs. "They made an impression last night, and of course, I want everyone to be a Rangers fan."

"But of course."

"Marry this guy," Jo-Joe whispers to me.

I shake my head. "It's not like that, Joe."

"Why not?"

"Because I barely know him better than you do."

"He's taking you out, isn't he?"

I shrug. There is no answer to his insightful point. "I'll see what I can do."

Deacon comes around and opens the passenger door. "You ready?"

"I guess so. Bye, guys." I hop into the passenger seat and slide on my seatbelt as Deacon closes my door. He fist bumps the guys and climbs into the driver's seat.

"Nice Jeep."

"A little more subdued than the Lambo, huh?"

"Just a little." I can feel his eyes on me as we wait at a red light up the street from my apartment building. "Yes?"

"You look pretty. Your look last night was intriguing, but your natural beauty really shines through right now."

"And the tattoos?" I quirk my brow.

"Oh, I have lots of questions." He smiles.

"Do you have any tattoos?" I match his smile, feeling no judgment radiating off of him.

"No. I wouldn't know what to get. I have surgery scars on my spine, but that's about it." We enter the parkway and head north. "What got you into tattoos?"

I lean back in my seat and watch the landscape fly by.

"I dated an artist for a while. He gave me my first couple, and I found the process very therapeutic."

"How so?"

Shrugging, I turn and stare at his face. He really is a beautiful man with sandy brown hair and hazel-green eyes, a chiseled jaw with the right amount of stubble on his cheeks. "The buzzing, the sting of pain, the satisfaction that a new piece of art is being embedded into my skin—it chills me out."

"Do you regret any of them?"

"No. They all meant something to me at one point or another. Even if I've grown and changed, the life lesson remains, and regretting them would be counterproductive to my spiritual growth."

Deacon says nothing, but the look on his face tells me he's impressed. We take an exit into Old Town. "Where are we going?"

"Mama Napoli. Have you ever been?"

"No."

He licks his lips and makes a show of patting his nonexistent belly. "It's a little hole in the wall on the west side. It's subdued and has the best food in town."

"If it's the best, why isn't it better known?" I challenge.

"Because the neighborhood is careful to not let their best kept secret loose into the world. Mama doesn't advertise. All of her business is word of mouth and has been for over forty years."

We get to the restaurant and park in the back. There is nothing flashy about the building, no valet opening our doors. I kind of love this side of Deacon because I know he could have easily taken me to the most expensive and exclusive restaurant in town. So, what does it mean that he took me somewhere low-key? Does he not want to be seen with me? Or does he not want his money to overshadow our experience?

When we enter, an older woman with dark hair and gray streaks comes out of the kitchen to wrap her arms around Deacon.

"Mama, this is London."

She smiles, her face warm and welcoming. "Welcome to my restaurant, London. We have your table ready in the back."

They escort us through the kitchen into a private dining room. Deacon pulls out my chair and then takes the seat next to me. "Like I said, best kept secret in town."

He pours me a glass of wine and then lifts his in a toast. "To overdue friendships."

We clink glasses, but I don't take a sip.

As I suspect, he notices.

"You don't drink," he states, rather than asks.

I shake my head.

He takes my glass and moves it to the other side of the table. "Okay, what would you like?"

"Water is fine for now. Sparkling water with lime is better."

"Easy enough." Deacon grabs the waiter's attention and has him remove the wine, replacing it with Pellegrino. Then he rattles off a couple of appetizers, like there are twelve versus two of us at the table.

Once the waiter walks away, I fold my fingers under my chin and stare at him, trying to peer past the nice guy routine to the truth beneath. "What are we doing here, Deacon?"

"What do you mean? We're having dinner." His brow furrows.

"I know, but why? Let's be honest, I'm not your type."

"How do you figure you're not my type? I mean, do I have a type?" He leans back in his chair and shakes his head. "I've dated white, black, and Hispanic women. Tall, short, blonde, brunette, and redheads. I don't know what my type is—so how could you know you're not it?"

I continue to stare at him, waiting until he cracks.

"All right, there is something I need."

"I knew it." I chuckle, because although I have no idea what someone like him would need from someone like me, I can't imagine anything coming out of his mouth will be *that* bad. He doesn't give me creep vibes, and my *jerk-face* radar is pretty on-point—finely tuned my sophomore year of high school.

He sighs. "I didn't start with it because I think it'd go a lot smoother if we were friends."

"You need a favor," I state, prompting him.

"Yes, and no. It would be a favor to me if you were my friend and wanted to do it. However, it would also be a business arrangement, and I'd make sure you're compensated accordingly."

"Does this have to do with massage therapy?"

"No, absolutely not. I got you an interview this week with my medical director—they should have called you, if not today, tomorrow. That is a legit offer regardless of this business opportunity. But—"

"What's this favor slash business opportunity?" He's rambling and I need him to cut to the chase because I'm getting anxious.

"You may know this, but I'm next in line to be general manager."

I nod. He's the only logical choice for the Rangers football team, especially since it is a family-owned franchise.

He sighs and continues. "Apparently my grandfather put special stipulations on the top positions. Namely, he wants to make sure the team always remains a family-run organization, and I can't take the GM position until I'm married."

I feel the color drain from my face. This is like driving up on a car accident. I'm horrified at the carnage coming up, but I can't turn away.

Is he really asking me to marry him? I can't say I've had a love-filled life. Most of my relationships have been absolute shit-shows, but the idea of marrying someone—actively entering a loveless marriage—makes me want to cry.

He chuckles and waves his hand as if to dissipate the negative energy filling the air between us. "I'm not asking you to marry me. Well, I'm not asking you to walk down the aisle with me. However, my father thinks if I was in a committed relationship with someone—say, a woman I went to high school with whom I'm head-over-heels in love with and desperately want to marry—maybe that would be good enough for my grandfather to allow me to take the GM position."

"A fake relationship?" I offer, just to make sure I'm understanding things correctly.

"A fake engagement," he clarifies.

"Why me?" I can't possibly be a fraction of the kind of girl Deacon Scott would marry. Looks, education, money, or pedigree—I don't have any of it.

He shrugs. "Honestly, I went to the reunion to see if I lost touch with someone I used to be cool with, but then quickly realized, no. I was never close to people in high school because, like you said, I was focused on what came next. I don't have a close girl—" he uses his hand to slash through the air "—friend I could ask to do this for me. You feel like someone I could be friends with."

There are worse things than forging a friendship with Deacon Scott, even if spending time with him might cause my lady bits to tingle late at night. He's hot—my mind wandering into no-man's territory for a minute or two last night before I put myself in check. He's way out of my league, so I guess I understand why he'd pick me to befriend in a purely platonic relationship.

I can't believe I'm even contemplating this. "How long are we talking?"

He sighs, as if he's been waiting for me to answer with bated breath. "Well, if it doesn't work, less than two weeks."

"And if it works?"

He shrugs. "I honestly don't know. As long as it takes for me to secure the GM position and get it officially announced. I'm thinking between six and eighteen weeks."

"Eighteen weeks!"

"The full season, longer if we go to the championship, and I'd want to introduce you this week, so let's say six months."

I stare at him as the server puts down three plates of appetizers—all mouthwateringly aromatic—and wait for him to say *Sike* or *Just Kidding* or *You've been Punk'd*. "What does this fake engagement consist of? Dating? Touching? Fucking?"

Deacon's stubbled cheeks flush, and his eyes grow wide as he chokes on a ravioli. "Jesus, London. You are no bullshit and that's why you're perfect. I'm sure there will be some social events we'll have to attend as a couple, but no, I wouldn't expect you to have sex with me. That's not public facing, and that's what this is about. Fooling the public, specifically, my grandfather, is what I'm trying to accomplish here."

I shove a forkful of calamari in my mouth, chewing thoughtfully for a minute. While this is one of the weirder days of my life, it's not the weirdest, and his request isn't awful. What else do I have to do? It's not as if my dating life is hopping at the moment. "What's in it for me, big boy? Why would I do this?"

"Why does anybody do anything? Money. You need it and I have it—so name your price."

"Well geez, Deacon, I wouldn't even know what to charge. It's not every day I get asked to be somebody's fake fiancée."

Play Action Fake

"How about twenty-five hundred dollars a week?"

My mouth opens and closes like a fish out of water. Twenty-five hundred a week? Potentially six months, twenty-six weeks, that's... "That's a lot of money."

He nods, his eyes searching my face. "And if I get the GM position, I'll double it at the end."

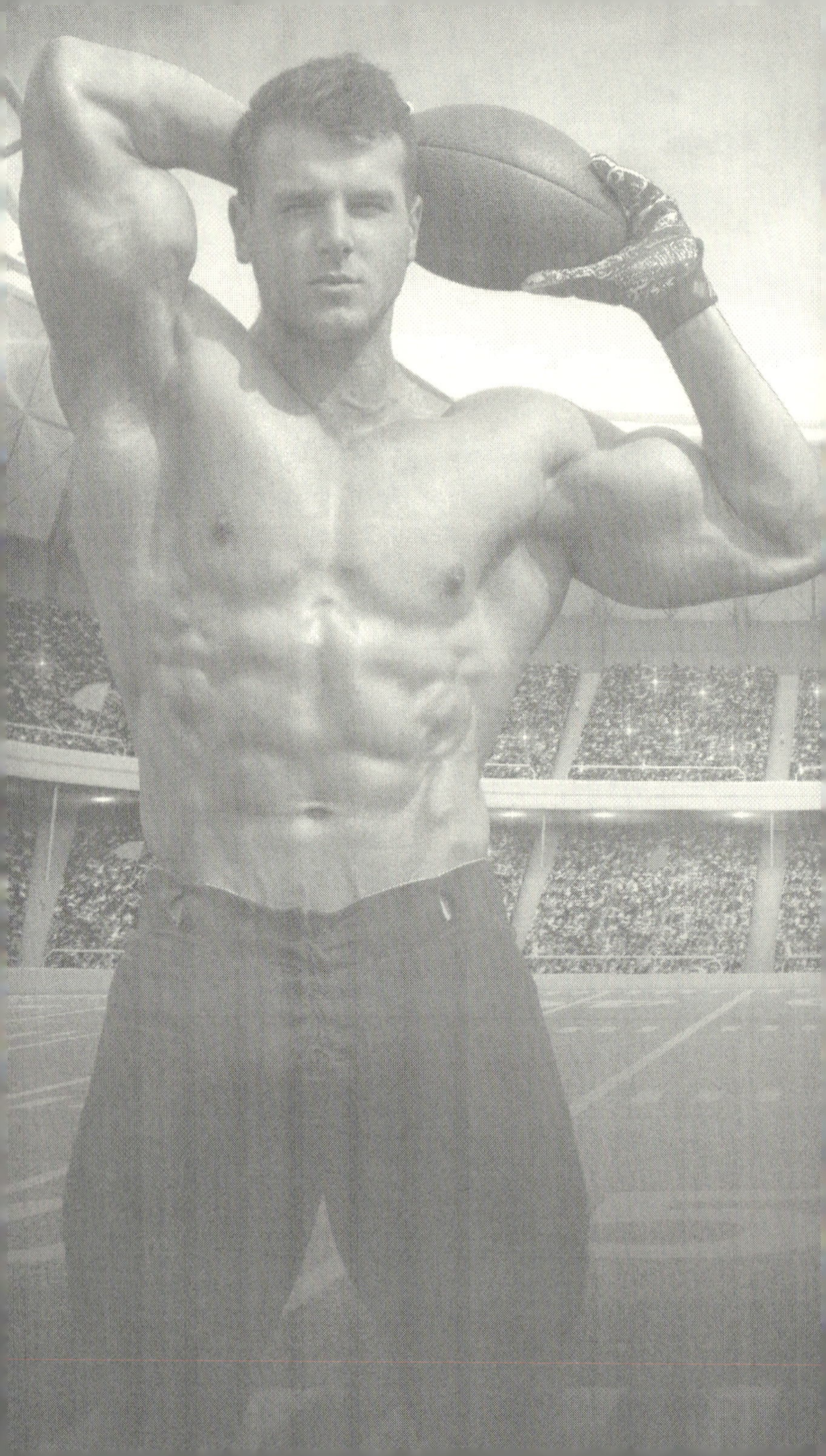

Chapter Five
Deacon

London and I have FaceTime'd every night for the last ten days, sometimes talking for hours. She's quickly become someone I can lean on—a genuine friend. Because she loves football, I can talk to her about my day without her eyes glazing over, which is a refreshing change from every woman I've ever dated. I've told her about my family, but I've noticed she's a lot more guarded with me about hers. No siblings. Her mother took off years ago and hasn't maintained consistent contact since she left. Her father is around, but that's all she has to say about him.

I pull up to her apartment building early, mostly because I expect to be waylaid by the three guys who are a fixture of the neighborhood. London said they ask about us every time they see her. Since there is a strong possibility my engagement will draw media coverage, I told her we should live the lie out loud, starting immediately.

To get that going, on Tuesday—my bi-monthly family dinner at my parent's house—I announced my intention to propose to my girlfriend, a woman of whom none of them knew anything about. To say there was pandemonium at the dining table is an epic understatement. My father pretended to be shocked while my mother was truly beside herself, and my grandfather stared at me while my brother and sister asked a million questions. My sister is three years younger than me while my brother is six years younger, so neither of them would remember London from school.

I fielded their questions, doing my best to sell the whirlwind romance she and I discussed. Honestly, London is a ride-or-die kind of chick, and I will do everything within my power to make sure this fake engagement is fun for her.

For us.

There's no reason to not enjoy ourselves while we live out this charade.

Of course, talking to her nightly and looking at her beautiful, sweet face while we chat about this or that, I have to keep reminding myself this is business—not a real romance—and falling for her is not an option. Deep feelings will muck up the works, but lucky for us, she seems unimpressed by me, keeping our conversations casual, which should make tonight interesting. I'm picking her up to take her to family dinner after supposedly proposing to her last Friday night.

Surprise! She said yes.

I climb the stairs, a bit surprised I haven't run into David, PB, or Jo-Joe, and knock at her door. This will be my first time in her apartment, which she seems reluctant to share with me.

"Hey." London flings open the door, and the attraction I'm suppressing comes rushing to the surface with one look at her.

"Holy shit." My jaw drops. She looks amazing in a soft pink form-fitting, long-sleeved dress with a black and pink shawl draped over the top, dark gray knee-high boots on her feet. Her hair is supple, pulled back from her face, and braided into a crown around her head.

"No good?" She casts a set of worried eyes down at her outfit. "I thought the pink would soften my look."

I take a step inside her apartment and close the door behind me. Crow, the black and white cat who constantly shoves his butthole into the camera during our FaceTime chats, meows as he saunters over to inspect me. "You look beautiful, London, but you don't have to change your look for me or my family."

"This is my look, too. I'm not always clad in black on black, and I rarely do my dark makeup unless I'm going out. We've talked on the phone every night for over a week. How often do I have makeup on?"

"That's true. You are a natural beauty." I can't stop myself from reaching out to cup her cheek. Her lips part —the physical attraction I thought one-sided returned to me with that simple gesture—which sends electricity trickling up my spine. "I just want you to know you don't have to change for me or my family. I like you the way you are."

She unwraps the shawl draped over her chest, revealing tattooed cleavage. "Is this too much?"

My brain temporarily disconnects, not because of the tattoos, but because she's so stacked, all that mouthwatering cleavage offered for a taste. "Uh…"

Giggling, she re-wraps the shawl around her shoulders. "Understood."

Holy hell. For the most part, London keeps her body covered, although no amount of cloth hides the fact that she's curvaceous.

I wonder if the tattoos are to detract from her luscious curves or accentuate them.

I jut out my elbow and offer my arm, waggling my brows and trying to ignore the intense desire coursing through my limbs that makes my fingertips itch to trace every dot of ink on her skin. "Come on. Let's go meet the family."

We pull up to my parents' house in Starlite Park. I take London's hand and slide a two-carat diamond engagement ring onto her finger.

"Wow." Her eyes are wide. "Being engaged to you looks good on me."

I laugh. "Everyone is here. So remember, we're deeply in love and can't keep our hands off each other."

"Can't keep our hands off each other?" She arches her brow.

"Well, it might come up. I guess we should've practiced."

"Practiced what, exactly?"

"Touching." I arch my brow at her smile. "Kissing."

Biting her lip, she puts her palm on my cheek and leans forward. "You think we should kiss?"

I suck in my breath at her nearness, the scent of her shampoo tickling my nostrils. Her breath caresses my face, making the blood rush to my dick.

Her eyes sparkle as she laughs and pulls back. "I took drama throughout high school, so I think I can act like I'm head-over-heels in love to fool the onlookers, but I'll keep my groping PG for the family."

Licking my lips, I exhale the breath I'd been holding and chuckle along with her. "You definitely fooled me."

"Have you set a date?" my sister, Deidre, asks London as she hands her a seltzer water with lime minus vodka.

I shake my head. "I know I rushed to put a ring on her finger, but with the pre-season starting this week, I don't think planning a wedding would be wise right now."

My mother, Linda, sits next to Deidre and chuckles. "Honey, it's cute that you think you'll be making important decisions about your wedding day."

"Uh..." Normally I'd call my mother out on declaring something *woman's work*, considering if any of the boys in the house said something like that, she and Deidre would slice us open with their sharp words. Instead, I opt to deflect the topic. "London will also be busy during the season."

"Why's that?" my grandfather asks from the armchair where he often holds court.

Don't get me wrong. My grandfather, Daniel Sr., isn't a horrible man, but he's rigid and set in his old ways and even older values. I'm sure London's tattoos are causing him to twitch. He bitches about overly tatted or pierced players during press conferences, but has learned to keep his mouth shut because it's a losing fight.

My father walks in to save me. "London is the medical team's newest staff member."

"You're a doctor?" my mom exclaims, a smile curling her lips.

"Massage therapist," London clarifies, and I watch as they exchange looks. There was a recent scandal on another team where a few of the players requested, and received, extra under-the-sheets treatment. To protect the women and players from any inappropriate conduct, real or imagined, they rarely use female massage therapists on several teams—ours included, until now.

"It's okay. Bob and I have talked, and they will do all treatments from all massage therapists in the open area of the physical therapy suite from now on, considering the recent press."

"That's good." My grandfather nods, his eyes cataloguing every inch of London's demeanor.

"Well, there's not enough time in the off-season to plan and hold a wedding, Deacon. We should hire a planner, and then you only have to meet with them a couple of times before the big day." My mom keeps going with the topic at hand—our impending nuptials.

"Right." Deidre nods. "Carrie hired Emily from Dream Weddings and says they've been great."

"So, now all we need is a timeframe." My mother casts her expectant gaze on me and London.

I slip my hand into London's, intertwining our fingers together, and bring our joined hands to my mouth, pressing a soft kiss on her delicate digits.

If we fight setting a date, red flags abound.

"What do you think, baby? Are you okay with a late spring wedding?" I look deep into her purple-gray eyes, thinking a baby with those irises would be striking and mesmerizing.

Her lips curve up at the end, her gaze fixated on our joined hands, which I hold up to my lips. "A spring wedding sounds beautiful."

"Would you be okay with turning over the planning to professionals?" Deidre blurts out.

London shrugs. "Sure."

"Then it's settled. I'll call the planners tomorrow and we'll go from there."

"What did I miss?" Declan walks into the sitting room with his phone in hand. His eyes widen as they land on London. "Oh, wow."

I raise my brow. "Bro?"

"Sorry. London, it's nice to meet you." He offers his hand, which means I have to drop hers.

She stands and shakes his hand. "It's nice to meet

you, Declan. I've been watching your career for so long, I feel like I know you."

"You know football?" He smiles at me.

"Does my girl know football?" I lean back onto the couch and smile. "Go ahead, baby. Amaze him."

She blushes, but Declan's grin, and the reaffirming tilt of his head makes her laugh. "Ranked in the top three across the league for the last five years, the changes implemented last year and resulting success between you and wide receiver Devlin Frank practically ensure you'll be the number one quarterback this year and probably MVP of the league. The offensive line is the strongest it's ever been with an average grade of 71.4 across the starting lineup. If the defense maintains its dominance this year, the Rangers can't be beat."

Declan glances over her shoulder at me, a big stupid smile on his face. "I like her."

"Yeah, me too." I roll my eyes.

"Do you gamble?" my grandfather pipes up.

"No, sir," London says, sitting back down next to me. I wrap my arm around her waist and pull her close, claiming and wordlessly cocooning her under my protection. "I don't have the money or inclination to waste it on things I can't control."

Shit. I really wish she hadn't brought up money.

My grandfather's eyes widen, but he says nothing.

"Well, I think I'll check on dinner." My mom claps her hands and stands up, breaking up the instant tension weaving itself throughout the room.

"How long do we have?" I call out, my eyes going to

London who sits there calm and unshaken. How she does it, I'm unsure.

"Maybe twenty minutes. Why don't you show London around the house, Deacon?"

It's like my mother knows we need a break. "Good idea."

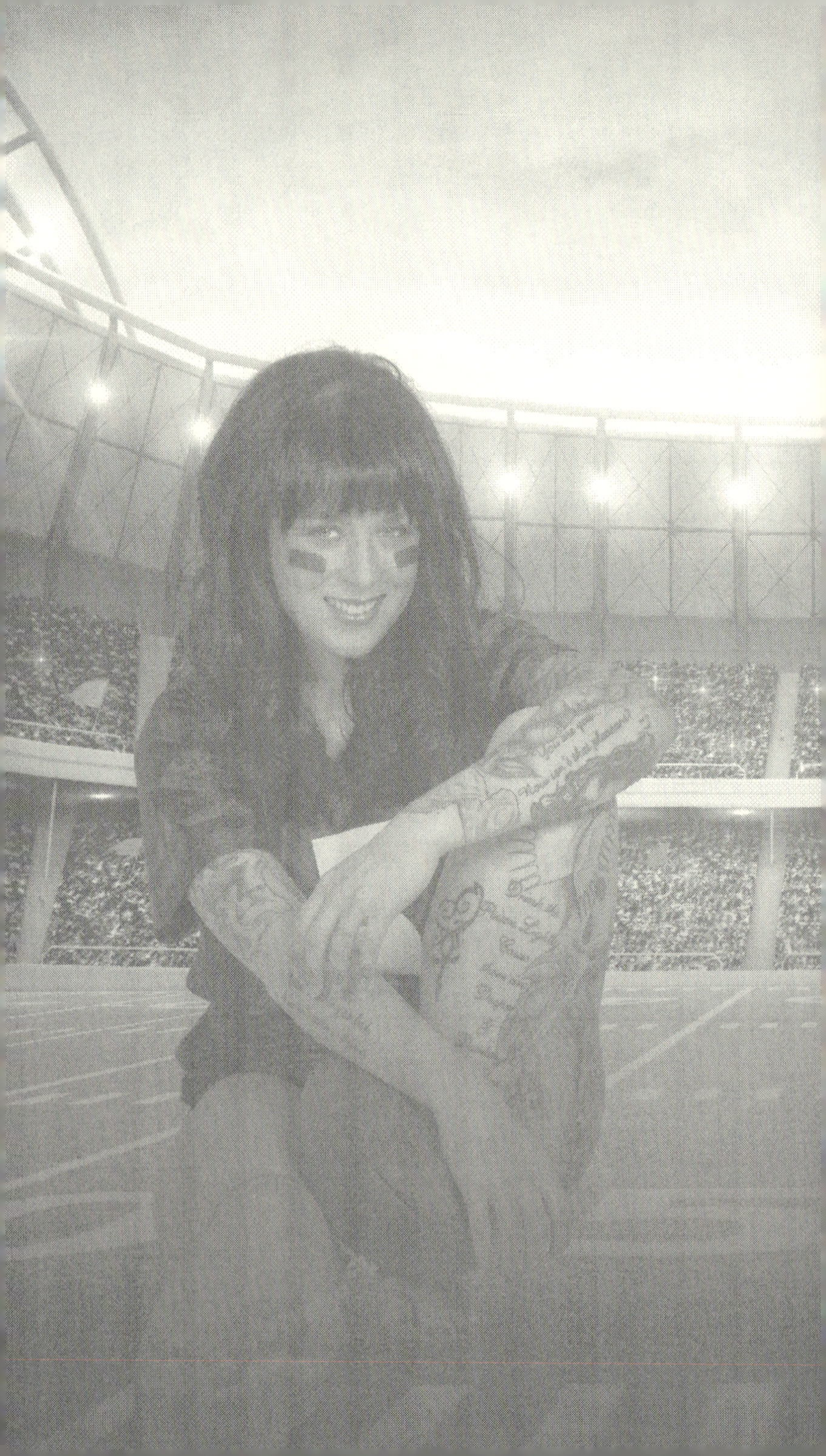

Chapter Six
London

We walk the grounds of his parents' mansion through a cultivated flower garden. It's beautiful, and the slight breeze in the air fills my lungs with the late summer blooms.

Deacon holds my hand like a man in love, his thumb brushing back and forth over my fingers, one of which has a gorgeous fake two-carat diamond ring on it. It has to be glass, but it's the prettiest ring I've ever seen. Not that I know diamonds, but this thing sparkles like nothing I've ever seen before.

"How are you holding up?" Deacon's voice is deep, rich, and soothing.

"I'm fine. Your family's nice. How far do we want to let the planning go before..." I'm not even sure how to finish that sentence. He will lose money planning a wedding that will never happen.

"If we slow-roll the planning, my family will know

something is up. No one gets engaged overnight and then wants to take their time getting married."

"Maybe we should say we eloped?" I offer. What's the difference between fake engagement and fake matrimony besides where we live—which currently is not together.

"After how excited my mom and sister got, I think eloping would break their hearts. I can't do that to them."

"But you can let them plan and then cancel a wedding?"

He shrugs. "Maybe my broken heart will inspire them to take it easy on me?"

His broken heart—that's funny.

"I think your grandfather is suspicious." I worry my lip as he stops at a bench near the fountain.

He sits down and pulls me onto his lap. "Yeah, me too, which is why I think I should do this."

Before I realize what he's doing, Deacon slides his big hand over the back of my neck and tilts my head up, claiming my lips with a possessive kiss I feel in my toes. He licks across the seam and I forget where we are as I gasp, granting him access to plunge deep and tangle with my tongue. I grip his biceps before running my hands into his hair, scraping my short nails against his scalp. "Oh, Deacon."

He pulls back and looks me in the eye, his hooded eyes drunk with lust that cannot be faked. "That felt real enough. Do you think it looked real to my grandfather watching us from the library?"

I exhale slowly, disappointment warring with elation

in my chest. I just got kissed by Deacon Scott, and even if it was for show, it felt too good to not manifest fantasies for later tonight. "If that doesn't make him a believer, I don't know what will."

It's been six weeks since I met Deacon's family and outside of a couple Tuesday night family dinners, I've spent more time with his mother and sister than I have him—the three of us having planning luncheons and girls' spa days quite a few times while Deacon, Declan, and their father Daniel are out of town with the team. Between his back office work, practices, and a full travel schedule, we've barely seen each other outside of our nightly chats.

I think we both felt something from that kiss in his family's garden because we've both been a little weird since then, tiptoeing around feelings and sticking to business which mostly revolves around the team and the GM position.

I love my new job with the Rangers and have found the players to be respectful, but also curious about me. Once news of Deacon's engagement hit the press, he made a point of coming to the medical facility a few times a week to drop in on me. But we're always surrounded by other people, so outside of a head nod or a peck on the cheek, we haven't had a minute alone.

My phone rings at nine p.m. Deacon is like clockwork, always prompt on his commitments, but never committing to things he can't control. He's yet to fail me, even if some of our conversations are cut short.

"Hello, handsome," I muse. I started calling him handsome after dinner with the family when he repeatedly called me baby, deciding a pet name was a smart habit to take on. We don't want to slip in front of his grandfather, whose ever watchful gaze is often on me.

So far, the ruse is working. We've kept Deacon's uncle and cousin out of the organization and focused on the Scott Real Estate Group, the family's other billion-dollar enterprise. Deacon hasn't been told he can take the GM position yet, but he hopes that's coming soon.

Really, there is no other choice.

"Hey, baby. How was your day?"

"Fine. It's quiet with the team out of town." It's Wednesday night, and Deacon, with the rest of the players, left this morning for tomorrow night's game on the east coast. They'll be home Friday afternoon and are taking a well-deserved weekend off. This will be their third game of the season, and they're expected to end the week at 3-0, the team even stronger than predicted during pre-season.

"I'm sure. You should travel with us once in a while."

"That's Travis's job." I shake my head. There are six full-time massage therapists on staff, only two of us specializing in trigger point therapy. Travis has been with the team for three years and loves the travel part of the job.

"Who says we can't have two traveling therapists?" Deacon turns away from the camera propped up on a countertop and pulls off his shirt. This isn't the first time he's gone shirtless in front of me, but my mouth waters and fingertips itch every time he does. Part of me wants to cat call him like some bachelorette party stripper—he's beautiful enough to pull in major cash via that alone—but I'm afraid he'd stop doing it and I definitely don't want that.

I've taken to wearing slightly more revealing PJs for our nightly calls. Initially, I wore long, baggy T-shirts and flannel pajama pants, but tonight I'm wearing a form fitting tank top with a low scoop neck and a pair of short shorts. I've also propped my iPad up on the coffee table, giving him an eyeful of more than just my face.

"Did you have lunch with mom and Deidre today?"

"Yes, and the wedding planner, Emily. I swear that woman could plan a lunar landing down to the minute."

He chuckles, his back to the camera. "What does our wedding look like right now?"

"So far I've kept it to under one hundred people, even though your sister says we're breaking protocol by not inviting the entire team. I compromised by selecting the ballroom at Castilla's Reserve which gives us room to grow. I'm pretty sure she thinks she'll wear me down after a while."

"Yeah, that's Deidre."

"Otherwise it is very elegant and understated. White and black attire with a hint of red for the team, of course."

"Of course. God forbid we do anything in this family that doesn't tie back to the team."

"Do you not want that? I guess it doesn't matter since

we'll be cancelling, anyway." I throw it out there, more to remind myself that this isn't real. Most days I forget because he makes my insides turn to jello on our nightly calls by being himself and nothing more.

He turns around to face the camera at the same time I shift on the sofa, my bare legs on full display. I know I've nabbed his attention by the way his eyes heat and his lips part, like he has something to say. "What are you doing Friday night?"

I shake my head, watching him crowd the camera to where I can only see his face and his shoulders, his hands out of view. "Nothing."

"Let's have dinner."

"Okay."

"At my house." His hazel eyes sparkle.

I quirk my brow. "Dinner at your place? That isn't in the public eye and does nothing to help sell this relationship, Deacon."

"Maybe I'm tired of putting on a show, London."

In my head I hear my inner voice—the one tired of fucking her vibrator night after night—scream, *Shut Up London*. But I can't leave his statement to my imagination and need him to clarify. "What does that mean?"

"I've been thinking about our kiss for six weeks, and I'm tired of wondering if I imagined the chemistry between us when our lips touched." He picks up the iPad and walks into his bedroom, putting it on the nightstand next to his bed. I watch as he pulls the sheets back, his ass clad in silky boxer shorts and that's it. The man is finely tuned, muscle upon muscle, which he keeps up by training with the team three days a week.

Now it's my turn to stare with my lips parted.

"And I know you've been thinking about it, too." He slips in between the sheets, letting the bleached white duvet rest low on his waist, and rolls toward the camera, propping his head up on his huge bicep.

His gaze caresses me through the camera, and my skin heats under his perusal.

"Tell me I'm wrong."

I lick my lips. "You're not wrong."

"We're friends, yes?"

"Yes."

"And mature adults."

I roll my eyes. "Sometimes."

He grins. "Take me into your room, London. Prop the iPad up on your dresser, and let me see this outfit you're teasing me with tonight."

I hesitate, my mind whirling with possibilities and implications. We're crossing a line, and I have no idea why tonight over any other night in the last six weeks.

Is this a bad idea? Probably.

Do I want to do it, anyway? Definitely.

Shit.

I pick up the tablet and walk into my bedroom, setting it up on my dresser like he told me to. Then I take several steps backward until my knees hit the mattress.

He hums his approval. "Very nice, London. Climb into bed."

I'm a little surprised by his bossiness. He's been an

absolute pushover since we met—always kind and attentive to my feelings. Not that he's being rude now, just authoritative and dominant. Is that how he is in bed? He's certainly that way with the players, as all good leaders should be, but now he's showing me a different side to him.

Still, I can't help but do what he says.

"Good girl."

I raise my brow. "You've never talked to me like this before."

"And it's been killing me not to. Do you want me to stop? Please say no." His hazel eyes look pain-filled and I'm wondering where else he feels discomfort. I'm imagining he's rock hard right now, and the idea that I've turned him on makes me warm and tingly, too.

"Don't stop."

"I've been fantasizing about the things I want to do to you for weeks. The way I really want to touch you when I only get a few seconds to turn it on for others. The things I want to do to you, London, aren't fit for the camera or public consumption." He sucks his bottom lip in between his teeth and then releases. "Do you have any fantasies involving me?"

My head spins with self-protection and lies, but my gut screams to tell him the truth. "Yes."

He smiles, but it's not friendly; it's predatory, and I know if we were in the same room right now, he'd have me pressed against a wall, his hands roaming all over me. "Do you touch yourself when you fantasize about me?"

"Oh, God, Deacon."

Play Action Fake

"That's a yes." He dims the light on the bedside table and then purposely slides his hand down his chest and under the duvet. "Would you touch yourself right now with me on the phone?"

My pussy clenches and my clit throbs with the idea. "Are we sure we want to take this step?"

He looks down at his erection off-camera. "Very sure. We won't film anything below the waist. I want to watch your face as you come tonight, because Friday night I plan to have my face buried between your legs."

My jaw drops open and a small blush warms my cheeks, but it's the rush of slick warmth trickling between my legs that truly has my attention. "I'm not good at dirty talk, Deacon."

"You don't have to be, baby. Just lie back, dim the lights, and imagine my touch as I caress you from head to toe."

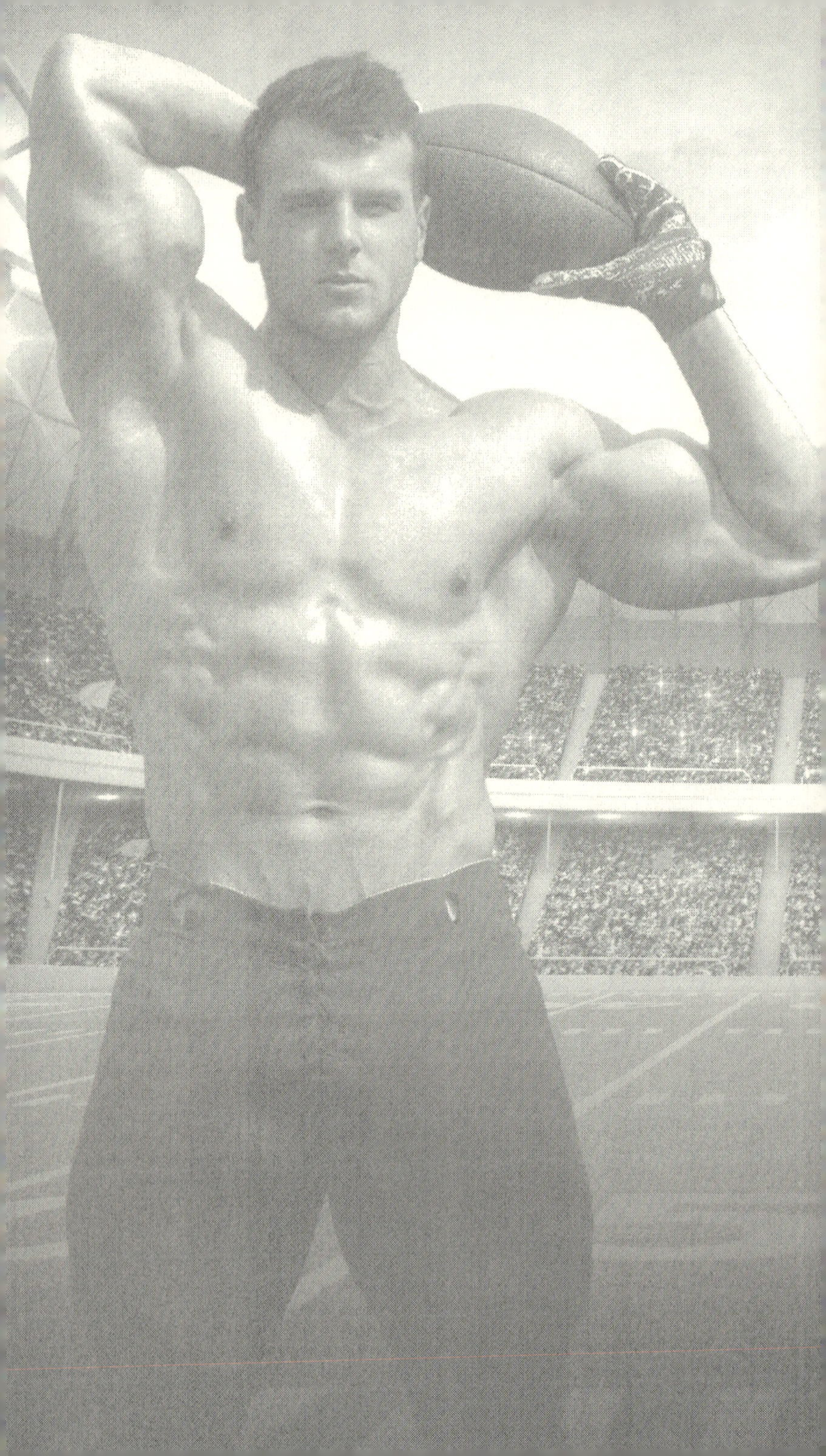

Chapter Seven
Deacon

One talk with my baby brother, and I'm crossing all carefully crafted boundaries and potentially blowing up six weeks' worth of fake relationship.

Declan cornered me on the plane and asked the hard question. "What's the real deal with London?"

I couldn't lie to my brother any better than I could to my father, so I told him about our grandfather's ludicrous rule in the bylaws and my business arrangement with London.

"But you like her," he stated rather than asked.

"I do."

"And you want her?" he stated again.

I made the mistake of bringing my eyes up to see the somber look on his face. Now I definitely can't lie to him. "Yes, I want her. Badly."

"Then what the fuck are you waiting for? Why have you shunned relationships your whole life? It doesn't have to be football or family, Deacon. You can have both."

"How much of our growing up was Dad absent for? I still don't understand why he and Mom are together."

"Dad's crafty. He makes Mom feel adored from afar—we just never saw it. If you like London, and you want London, you might find you love her, too, but you won't know until you move whatever this is from the practice field to live scrimmage—and if you wait too long, you'll lose her."

I cast him a questioning raise of my brow. "Declan, you are the biggest manwhore the Scott family has ever claimed as their own. Where do you get off talking to me about love?"

"If anyone knows about fucking up love, it's me. You've avoided it your whole life while I've chased and scared it away—often."

That was several hours ago and now I'm FaceTiming London, watching as bright pink color tint her cheeks. "I'm not good at dirty talk, Deacon."

I growl low in my throat. "You don't have to be, baby. Just lie back, dim the lights, and imagine my touch as I caress you from head to toe."

She bites her lip. "Hold on one second." Jumping out of bed, London crosses out of frame. The overhead lights go dark, and a small light source comes on from behind the camera, casting the room in red, then pink to purple to blue. She jumps back into bed and pulls the covers over her belly, turning to face the camera and ultimately me.

A small, shy smile spreads across her lips as words escape her. But that's okay. She doesn't need to speak because I have more than enough to say.

"You know what my number one fantasy featuring you has been?"

"What?"

"I desperately want to lay you out on a massage table in the middle of the medical center and plunge my tongue deep into your pussy. The image of you with your scrub bottoms pooled around your feet as I push your thighs wide so I can fuck you with my mouth gets me so worked up that every time I visit you in the training facility, I'm rocking a hard-on."

"Oh, wow." Her voice is breathy—hot and erotic—and I can imagine her words vibrating against my ear as I hover over her, pumping my cock in and out of her hot pussy.

"Touch yourself for me."

She flashes me a devious smile. "Only if you touch yourself at the same time."

I turn the camera slightly so she can see my hand moving underneath the sheets. "Baby, I've been stroking myself since you got on camera and flashed me your bare legs."

"Do you want to know what fantasy I've had running through my head for the last few weeks?" she says as she slides her hand up her stomach to cup her breast. She flexes her fingers, kneading her cotton-covered flesh, before pinching and rolling her peaked nipple between her thumb and forefinger.

Watching her makes my mouth water. "What, baby?"

"I've fantasized about being your center, bent over in front of you with my legs spread wide, feeling you fill me over and over again with each thrust of your hips."

"Fuck—and you said you couldn't dirty talk. I can't wait to get my hands on you Friday night."

"I'll wear a jersey if you like," she teases.

"You'll wear my jersey and only my jersey from now on. Now slide your hand between your legs and rub your clit." I tighten my grip on my cock—the slow, languid strokes no longer doing it for me. I've come so many times with thoughts of London over the last few weeks, I'm surprised I've held it together this long. Not getting to spend time alone with her has certainly helped me keep my hands to myself, but one half-ass talk with my brother, and my tethered control has finally snapped.

"How wet are you?"

"Soaked."

"That's what I want to hear. I'll have you gushing soon enough. Rub tiny circles for me, and imagine my tongue lapping up your juices."

She rolls to her back, her head tilted toward me as her eyes close. Seconds tick by as I whisper words of encouragement, telling her how beautiful she is, and how hard I come when I think about her in the shower. Her lips part as her chin juts into the air and her breasts reach for the ceiling, the soft moans coming out of her mouth turning harsh as she curses.

"Oh fuck. Deacon. Fuck."

That's all I need to hear to take my balls from tight to

exploding as I come into my boxer shorts, pearly drops spilling over my fist.

One Thursday game won and a restless night later, we've landed in Denver and are driving down to Spring City.

"You going out with London tonight?" Declan says without looking up from his cell.

"I'm picking her up on the way to my place." We played on the phone last night too, proving Wednesday night wasn't a fluke. If she's nervous about seeing me, I plan to kiss that out of her the moment she opens her door. Now that I've unshackled my heart—and my cock—I'm over the moon excited to see her, touch her, explore and devour every inch of her until neither of us remembers our names. I like everything I know about her and have a million more questions—my desire to be her friend, her lover, her everything consuming me to the point of insomnia.

My father, who normally doesn't travel with us, perks up. "You're going out with London?"

"Yeah."

"I thought you were..." His brow furrows, and his eyes dart to Declan before coming back to me.

"It's cool. Declan knows all about London."

He frowns. "Who else knows?"

"Just the three of us."

My father raises the privacy divider between us and

the driver. "Although we never discussed details, I thought this was a business arrangement to get the GM position. Don't tell me this poor girl thinks you're actually going to marry her."

Declan puts his phone down, his eyes wide as they bounce between me and our father.

"It is a business arrangement, but I also like her."

"Like her?" His tone is full of doubt.

I clench my jaw and narrow my eyes. "Care for her. Why? What's the problem?"

My father takes in a deep breath, letting it out slowly. "Your grandfather doesn't care for her. He's leery of her and the threat she represents to this family."

"What the fuck are you talking about? What threat?"

"Her father is an alcoholic, and her mother is an addict and a gambler. We can't have that associated with the Scott family or this football team."

I figured there was alcoholism somewhere in her gene pool, considering she doesn't drink—which, to me, only highlights how exceptional she is as a person. The gambling is a minor problem, but considering she hasn't spoken to her mom in years, I don't see the big deal. "How the hell does he know that?"

"He had her investigated."

Growling, I shake my head and cast my eyes to the floorboards. "That's infuriating, but I fail to see the problem."

"You should know your grandfather is considering offering you the GM position if you dump London."

"He's rewriting the bylaws?"

"He's making an exception."

Just then my phone buzzes with an incoming text, London's name flashing on my screen.

> I received a package from you. Should I open it or wait until you get here?

After seeing her in her skimpy tank and short set, I felt inspired to do a little shopping, having a couple sets of sexy, silky sleepwear ordered from a lingerie shop. Phil helped me out and ensured me they'd be delivered before I arrived home this afternoon.

> Don't open it until tonight.

> See you soon?

> I should be there in forty minutes.

I stuff my phone back into my pocket and bring my eyes up to my father and brother. Anger wars within me, and I resent being manipulated for a position I damn well deserve. Taking the general manager position is best for me, for the organization, and for the family—so why are they fucking with me about my personal life?

"And what did you say?" I pose the question to my father. "Do you think it's okay for him to dictate who I date and when? What if I was gay? Would he write me out of the family will if I was in love with a man?"

"Deacon, don't be ridiculous." My father sighs and leans back in his seat, but I won't be placated. Not this time.

"I'm fucking serious, Dad. Who the fuck is he to tell me who I can and cannot date, marry, or fuck?"

"I didn't think you were serious about her, so I didn't object when he brought me his concerns."

"And if you had known how serious I am?"

My father deflates, which is all the answer I need. I love my dad, but he's always cowered to his father. Well, that stops now.

"I am the best candidate to replace you, but my personal life is not up for discussion."

"You're willing to give up the GM position for her?"

"I don't know that yet. What I do know is that I'm unwilling to make decisions about who I love for a job."

Both my father and brother stare at me as we pass through the security gate onto the property, and although I know I used the L word, I'm not clarifying my point because it remains the same. Am I in love with London? I don't know, but I feel stronger about her than I have any other woman I've ever dated. I haven't taken the time to get to know a lot of women—the Scott name and quarterback fame always preceding me as a person in their eyes. With London I've established a friendship, as well as a physical attraction. Isn't that what a relationship is all about?

As soon as the driver stops the car, I've opened the door and signaled to the driver to pop the trunk. I've got my bag in hand and am walking to my car before my dad can say a word to stop me.

I text London as I'm driving off the property.

Play Action Fake

> I'll be at your place in twenty minutes.

> You're early!

> Yeah. See you soon.

Time to see what kind of relationship she wants to have with me and if this is long-term—like, forever?

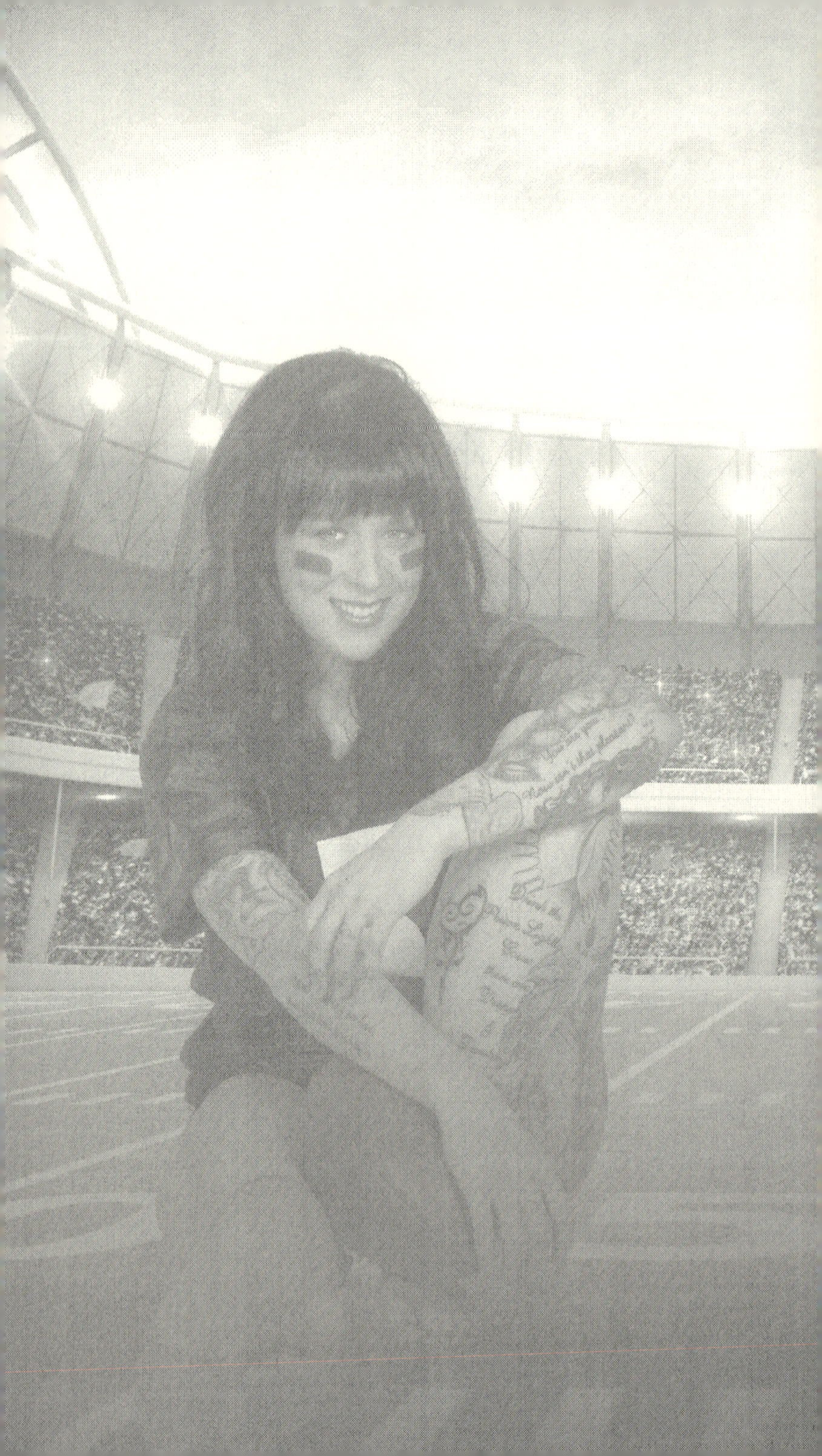

Chapter Eight
London

Butterflies dance a jig in my stomach as I watch Deacon pull up to the apartment complex in his Range Rover. He briefly says hello to the guys, but he's on a mission, because he waves them off as he disappears inside my building.

I have my overnight bag packed and I'm opening my door when Deacon rounds the corner and fills my doorway with his larger-than-life presence.

"Hi!" I squeak as Deacon grabs the bag and tosses it to the floor, kicking the door shut behind him. In two steps, he has me in his arms and is lifting me off the ground, my only response to wrap my legs around his waist and hold on for dear life. He presses me against the closest wall and claims my lips with a kiss that lights up every nerve ending in my body. Slick arousal floods my panties as he presses into me and shifts his hips, his cock hard, large, and ready to impale me.

I pant as he lets my lips loose to trail kisses down my

neck, one big hand palming my breasts. "You really are beautiful, London. You know that?"

"I'm picking up the hint." I tug on his hair, trying to snatch his attention. Not that I don't love his hands on me, and being picked up and taken against a wall fulfills so many of my fantasies, but I feel like there's something wrong. "Everything okay?"

He brings his hazel eyes to mine. "I need to be inside of you."

I smile. "I need you inside of me."

"I live twenty minutes from here and have catering coming in thirty."

"So, you're saying we have ten minutes to fool around?"

"That isn't long enough for what I want to do to you, so let's go."

He sets me down on my feet and takes my hand, walking over to my bag and hoisting it on his shoulder. "Is Crow going to be okay by himself tonight?"

"He'll be fine."

I lock up my apartment and follow him down the stairs, taking his hand again as we exit the building. The guys are standing there with huge, goofy, knowing smiles on their faces.

"Awww, yeah." Playboy elbows David, who turns his beet-red face away from us.

"Bye guys." I shake my head.

"Bye London!" Jo-Joe yells in a sing-song voice way louder than necessary.

Play Action Fake

Deacon holds open my door while tossing my bag into the back. "What are you guys doing next Sunday?"

The guys exchange a look and shrug.

"I'm going to arrange for you three to hang with London in my private box at the stadium for our game against the Denver Mustangs. Can you clear your schedules?"

"Oh, my god! Are you serious, man?"

"Yeah, and each one of you can bring one guest, so make it someone cool you want to impress."

My heart swells as the guys jump up and down. Deacon closes my door, fist bumps them, and then slides into the driver's seat.

"That's so sweet," I say.

"They watch over you, so I owe them for taking care of my girl when I'm not around."

"Your girl?"

"Yeah." He turns to face me with a salacious grin, his eyes heated as he looks me up and down. "Mine."

I have nothing to say to that, my insides turning into molten goo. No man has ever claimed me as his, even if he introduced me with lackluster enthusiasm as his girlfriend. In thirty-three years, I've never felt the level of possessiveness Deacon has rocked in the last few days.

What changed?

Do I care?

Deacon calls the catering company on the way to his house, instructing them to leave the food on the counter and get out. I guess we'll be eating later tonight. Good thing I'm not hungry.

He lives in a secluded house with a mile-long driveway that winds its way up a private hilltop. We park in the garage and walk through the house, my hand firmly held by his.

"I'll give you a tour later," he says as we climb a wood staircase to the top floor. The house is beautiful, but it's sterile, as if furnished by an interior designer and maintained by a cleaning staff. It doesn't feel lived in or loved at all.

Actually, it feels hollow and lonely, which makes my heart break for the man holding my hand.

Does the house reflect the man?

"This is beautiful." We walk into an expansive bedroom with floor-to-ceiling windows facing the mountains in the west. The massive bed is obviously handmade and tailored to his six-foot-four frame. Like the rest of the house, it has a sterile feel, everything dustless and perfectly placed—photograph-ready. "How long have you lived here?"

"A couple years."

"Really?"

He looks around, placing our bags on the ground and my unknown gift on the bed. "I'm not home much."

"What did you get me?" I finger the department store bag with fancy tissue paper to change the topic.

Play Action Fake

Deacon shrugs out of his jacket, tossing it to a chair, and kicks off his shoes, a wicked smile on his face. "Open it."

I also kick off my shoes and pull a beautiful box out of the bag—Lindy's Lingerie embossed on the top. I pull the top off and peel back the paper to reveal black and purple silk and lace material—not Rangers team colors.

"Your outfit inspired me the other night. I like the idea of talking to you while you're wearing something—" he walks up behind me, already shirtless with the buttons of his pants undone, and slides his hands around my waist, kissing my neck "—inspirational."

Closing my eyes, I lean into his chest and reach behind me, sliding my hands up his thighs and over his erection.

He sucks in his breath, gathering up the hem of my shirt and pulling it over my head. Then he spins me to face him, sliding one hand into my hair, pulling my head back and kissing me deeply. In a matter of seconds, he's got both of us naked and has me spread out underneath him on his plush mattress.

"I wonder how many times you'll come for me?" he murmurs as he moves his way down my body, nipping at my skin with small love bites.

I'm wondering that myself considering I'm on the brink of releasing right now. He has me so worked up—I've been on edge for a week—and the nightly dates with my vibrator haven't sated me. "I'll come as many times as you make me, handsome."

"I like the sound of that." Deacon lifts my thigh up

over his shoulder, spreading me wide. He blows softly across my slick pussy and then presses another bite onto my inner thigh. "I have this overwhelming desire to bite you, mark you as mine."

"I have no reason to hide the marks you gift me."

He clamps down harder on the tender flesh of my upper inner thigh, making me cry out. That one is going to leave a mark.

He lets go and then buries his mouth against my pussy, plunging his tongue deep into my cunt, lapping and sucking on my clit until I'm writhing underneath him, rolling my head from side to side and chanting his name.

My first orgasm hits quickly, but it's followed by a second harder orgasm that has me cursing and pushing his head away.

He's chuckling as I come back to myself, his touch light and soothing as he waits for my brain to reconnect with my body.

"Holy shit!" I pant.

"I like the way you come, baby."

"That was intense."

Deacon slides his fingertips over my swollen pussy, slipping two fingers inside. His touch is gentle, his body shaking with restraint. Slowly, he pumps his fingers in and out of me until I'm involuntarily riding his hand, begging for more.

"Fuck me, handsome."

"Are you ready for my cock, baby?"

"Please."

Deacon climbs up my body, lavishing my nipples before kissing my lips, his heavy cock probing my entrance. "You never have to beg me to pleasure you, London. It's mine to do anytime you want."

"I want."

Grinning, he thrusts his hips forward and fills me with one smooth stroke, stretching me wide.

I gasp, my pussy throbbing as I adjust to his size, another orgasm threatening to spill over.

"Fuck, you are tight. I can feel your next release coming."

"Fuck me, Deacon. Please fuck me hard and fast," I whine, wanting him to claim me by making me sore and bruised. I want to have the memory of him pumping in and out of me long after we climb out of this bed. Is this a one-time thing or more? I don't know, but I know I never want to forget what it feels like having Deacon Scott touch and use my body for his pleasure while giving me pleasure in return.

His hips jackhammer into me as he chases his release. The grunts and groans coming from his lips buried against my neck turn me on more. I clutch at his wide shoulders, digging my nails into his skin as another orgasm crests over the edge, my cunt clamping down on him like a vice while he spills his seed inside of me.

Deacon's heavily muscled body sags on top of me for a second as he pants to catch his breath. Then he rolls to my side and pulls me with him, his hand cupping my knee and pulling my thigh over his hip.

He strokes my cheek and brings his hazel eyes to mine. "This wasn't supposed to get complicated."

"How did it get complicated?" I bite my lip and stare back at him, mesmerized by the content look on his face. Is this his way of telling me this is just sex? I can't say I wasn't expecting it. He's Deacon Scott and I'm nobody other than a cool chick filling a role for a limited time. His family is nice enough, and his sister is working hard to establish an actual relationship with me—one I'm trying to hold off on forming since eventually this will all come crashing down—but I don't really belong in their world and I know it.

"I don't want to pretend anymore, London. I want this with you. I want a real relationship."

Okay, I wasn't expecting that at all. I was hoping for it, but never expecting it. "You do?"

He nods and brushes the hair back from my face. "I don't know how to be a boyfriend. I've never seriously dated a woman while maintaining my responsibilities to the organization and the team."

Leaning forward, I lie my head against his giant pec, my ear pressed against his thumping heart. Staring in his eyes is too intense, especially as I make my claim on him. "Any woman who dates you has to understand the time and dedication the team requires, especially during the season. Obviously, I'm going to want sex often because that was so good..."

He chuckles, his chest vibrating under my cheek.

"Maybe we can establish a recurring date night, but I

don't see why you can't seriously date a woman—specifically me."

"If you lived with me, I could come home to you every night," he murmurs.

I lift my face to look him in the eye. "That's moving pretty fast. Are you sure that's what you want?"

"We are engaged, London, and have been together for six weeks."

"But it's not a real engagement."

"It could be. The ring is real. The wedding planning is real. I think deep down, I knew before I laid eyes on you that you were the one. You were the only person I thought of as soon as this crazy idea came into my head. How's that possible, considering we'd barely met before the reunion, if not a stroke of destiny?"

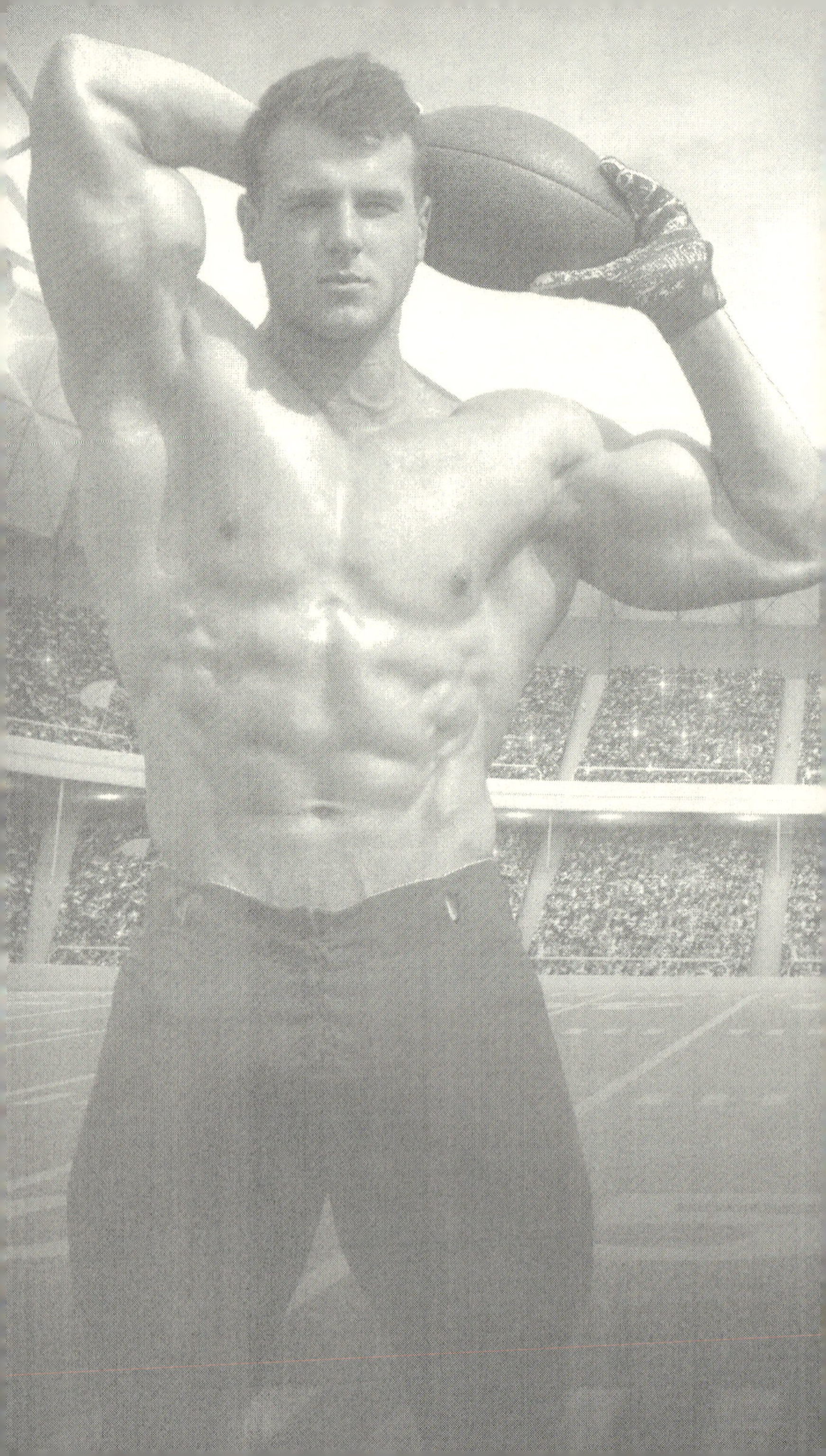

Chapter Nine
Deacon

I've never felt such intense feelings for a woman before, deep knowledge that she's the one settling in my gut. I learned when I was young to follow my instincts because they never fail me, but something tells me I'm freaking London out right now.

Can I blame her?

"The ring is real?" Her furrowed brow is more telling than her words.

"You thought it was fake?"

"I thought it was the most beautiful piece of glass I've ever seen."

I snort. "Oh no, baby. I don't know why, but I didn't think to buy a fake diamond. That's a two-carat, VVS1, near-colorless diamond set in platinum, and it's yours if you want it."

She brings her hand up and wiggles her fingers. "Holy shit, Deacon! I've been tossing this thing around like it was silver and glass, and not twenty thousand dollars' worth of jewelry."

I shrug, the price tag the least of my concerns. What's important right now is that she understands the business portion of our relationship is complete, so we can focus on the genuine feelings growing between us. "Have you checked your bank account since Wednesday?"

"No."

"I paid you all twenty-six weeks because I didn't want money exchanging hands while we did this for real."

"But if it's real, why would you pay me at all?"

"I'm severing our business arrangement, which means I owe you the full amount."

"I don't remember that being part of our agreement."

"In my head it was."

London slides her hand down my chest and trails her fingers softly over my semi-hard cock. "I guess paying me while we have sex would make this weird."

"That, and I don't want you to feel you have to stay with me. The money is yours. The ring, yours. Now, if you're with me, it's because you want to be."

She wraps her fingers around me and strokes my fully roused cock, causing my hips to arch into her touch. "I want to be with you, Deacon. I'm crazy about you and way more invested than I thought I could be with anyone, ever."

I cup her face and kiss her with every ounce of passion and gratitude running through my body. She straddles me and lowers her hot, wet pussy onto my aching cock, riding me slowly. Filling her feels so good. It sends tingles up my spine as she moans her need.

"You fill me perfectly, Deacon."

Pressure builds in my balls, and I know I'm not going to last much longer. "Lean back, baby. Let me play with your clit."

She arches her back and grabs her ankles, this new angle hitting her spongy g-spot perfectly. With a little pressure from my thumb, it takes nothing to push her over the edge, this time a guttural growl escaping her lips as her pussy pulses around me.

I release deep inside her again, the potential consequences of our unprotected sex smacking me in the face. I'm never careless, always wrapping up before engaging, and yet with London I didn't even think twice—as if having her swollen with my child is my number one priority.

She collapses on my chest, panting for breath. I smooth her hair back and tuck my fingers under her chin, lifting her face so I can claim her lips again. "Are you on birth control, baby?"

"I am."

To my surprise, disappointment bubbles in my belly. Was I really hoping she'd get pregnant and carry my child? "Do you want kids someday?"

"Honestly, I haven't thought about it."

I think about her relationship with Jo-Joe, Playboy, and David, and while she said they keep her safe, she also nurtures them in her own way.

"I think you'll be a great mom." Planting the seed, I leave the conversation for another time.

"Do you want kids?" she asks.

"Someday." I can't say I've thought about it a lot either, but I've always liked kids and love our summer camps when we invite underprivileged kids to the practice field for a couple days of horsing around. "Are you hungry?"

"Starved. We've worked up quite an appetite."

Chuckling, I smack her ass lightly, noting how her eyes light up. Hmmm. She likes a bit of the rough stuff. I can't wait to find out how rough. "You want to take a shower first?"

"Yes. Then I can show off some of my skill, too." She swings her leg over and kneels beside me on the bed.

"Skill?" I raise my brow as I sit up.

"Skills I keep hidden." She bites her lip and looks down. "Do you really not know what Joe Hyland was insinuating at the reunion?"

Shit. I forgot all about that. "I didn't until you ran out of there, then I asked him about it. He didn't say who—I didn't ask—but I know they tormented you for some dumb shit that, as soon as I heard it, knew couldn't be true."

"It wasn't dumb, it was devastating. Tiff Wilson was my best friend until the summer before our sophomore year, when her mother married Jennifer Combs' father and they became step-sisters. That summer, they vacationed together, bonded, and Tiff entered tenth grade as one of the cool kids. She's the one that made up the rumor, but as you know, most rumors have a hint of truth to them. I was at the party that night, and I did get drunk—passing out on Tiff's bedroom floor after Mark Maine tried to kiss me poolside. Tiff had a huge crush on him. She was so mad about the almost kiss, she unleashed her venom and ruined my high school experience. When I woke up, I learned I'd gone down on three guys, one after another. It wasn't true, of course, but I couldn't prove it since everyone had seen me fall down drunk." London worries her hands. "My father is an alcoholic and my mother is an addict, so after that night I knew if I didn't want to follow in their footsteps, I couldn't touch another drop or experiment like a normal teen. I'm as straight-edged as you can get without including religion."

Rubbing her thigh with one hand, I wrap my fingers around the back of her neck with my other, and wait until she makes eye contact. "I'm sorry that happened, London. I wish I would have protected you."

She smiles and shakes her head. "Don't apologize for the past, but if we're going to have a future, I need to put all my cards on the table. I'm guarded. I have the tiniest inner circle. And I have carefully negotiated my sexual exploration. I wouldn't go down on my boyfriends because the rumor gave me a mental block, but then I learned how empowering it is to have someone's sex in my mouth, their pleasure controlled by me."

I pull her lips up to mine, kissing her gently. It fucking kills me that anyone ever hurt her, but that will never happen again. I won't allow it. From now on, she's mine to protect, even if it is from my family. "I want you always to be open and honest with me, London. You can tell me anything—your likes, dislikes, desires, and needs—and if I can fulfill them, I will. Let me love you."

"Only if you let me love you, too." There are tears in her smoky gray eyes as I pull her close.

"I'm all yours, baby."

It's Tuesday night and we're at my parent's house. I haven't spoken to my father since the ride home on Friday, except to let him know we would be at dinner tonight. The first person we see as we walk through the front door is Declan, who arches his brow in question.

I bring London's hand to my mouth and kiss her fingers as my answer.

Declan smiles and raises his glass, letting me know where he stands on this topic.

My mother and sister are in the kitchen, bickering over something while my father walks out of the library, a somber look on his face. He greets us with a subtle nod of his head. "London, Deacon."

"Dad?" I respond. If this is going to be a thing, I'd rather get it over with.

He sighs and motions to the study. "Your grandfather wants to talk to you both."

I tense and my jaw clenches. Part of me wants to keep London from my grandfather, so she doesn't have to deal with him. If he's nasty to her—so help me, God—I won't be able to bite my tongue. I'd prefer she didn't know about his feelings and stay blissfully unaware, but before I can take her to the kitchen, my grandfather is at the door smiling at us. "London, so nice to see you. Come talk to me."

I narrow my eyes and tighten my grip on her hand.

She casts me a raised brow, silently asking me what's wrong.

Shaking my head, I murmur low enough so only she hears me. "I'm sorry."

We follow Daniel Sr. into the study where he takes up residence in the leather wing-backed chair behind the oversized black walnut desk. He motions to the two chairs facing the desk. "Have a seat."

"We'd rather stand," I say plainly.

"Suit yourself." My grandfather shrugs. "I know this relationship is a sham and you're only doing it for the general manager's position. Even if you have developed feelings for each other, they are new and fleeting and destined to fade given your very different backgrounds. Instead of dragging your family and the media through this farce of a relationship, we can use the announcement of my retirement, and you and your father's subsequent role changes to hide the dissolution of your engagement."

London's eyes are wide, but she's smart, because instead of engaging my grandfather, she's looking to me to answer.

"Yeah, you're right. This started because of the general manager position and the ridiculous rule you have in the bylaws, but I guess I should thank you because, had it not been for that rule, I wouldn't have found London, gotten to know her, and fallen in love." I bring her hand up to my mouth again, kissing her fingers, hoping to convey my love and commitment with my eyes.

I see her body visibly relax. She smiles and leans into me as her response.

"And you're committed to London?"

"Yes."

My grandfather turns his eyes on her. "I'm sure you're in love, London, but is this relationship worth potentially stripping Deacon of the right of owning the Rangers or leaving the team all together?"

"Don't answer that," I say as she shakes her head.

"I want to answer it." She smiles and turns to face him. "I would never hurt Deacon, and therefore, the choice is his. However, I will stand by his side no matter his decision, even if it breaks my heart."

My grandfather arches his brow. "If you care so much about him, you'll take the burden of this decision off him and walk away with whatever compensation you require, letting him take on the general manager position."

She takes in a deep breath and lets it out slowly. "Whatever your problem is with me, it would be stupid for you to force his hand and allow the organization to suffer without his leadership, but again, that's on you. Don't put it on me. It's your burden to bear should you force him out because he chooses me."

My grandfather, the man who keeps his emotions in check and has for all my life—probably my father's too—laughs. An honest to goodness genuine laugh, his face transformed by a huge smile as his gaze bounces between us. "No one other than my wife has ever talked to me like that."

"Sorry, but not sorry." London shrugs and holds her ground.

I have to say, I'm even more turned on by her right now. She's ballsy, and beautiful, and a perfect mate for me, and I want nothing more than to blow off dinner and take her back to my bed.

Our bed—as soon as I can get her moved in with me.

"Well, if that's all..." I wrap my arm around London's waist and turn to leave.

"That's not all." Daniel Sr. stands up and rounds the desk to face us, offering London his hand. She looks at me and then lets go of my hand, giving it to him. He pulls her into his arms. "I'm sorry I misjudged you, London. The Scott legacy is very important to me, and I wanted to make sure you were a good fit, which you obviously are with that kind of spirit. Welcome to the family."

My protective instincts roar as I brace myself to intervene, but London wraps her arms around him, and the old man melts.

Damn, now I'm even more impressed.

My father pokes his head into the study to survey the scene. His eyebrows shoot up as he makes eye contact with me.

I shrug, completely at a loss of an explanation.

"Dinner's ready," he says, walking fully into the room.

"Great." Daniel Sr. pats my shoulder and nods, conveying to me wordlessly a truce of sorts. What that truce is comprised of, I don't know. Time will tell, I guess, but I'm willing to get through this dinner to keep the peace.

In a few brief minutes, London has proven my instincts right. She's my rock, my ride-or-die chick, and my friend. My heart swells as we're left alone in the study, my grandfather following my dad to the dining room.

"I'm sorry about that." I pull her into my arms and kiss her temple, wrapping my arms tightly around her body.

"Do me a favor, Deacon."

"What's that, baby?"

"You asked me to be open and honest with you—well, I ask the same. Don't give up something that you'll one day resent me for."

"I'm not giving up anything, especially you. I love you, London."

Her grayish-purple eyes tear up. "I love you, too."

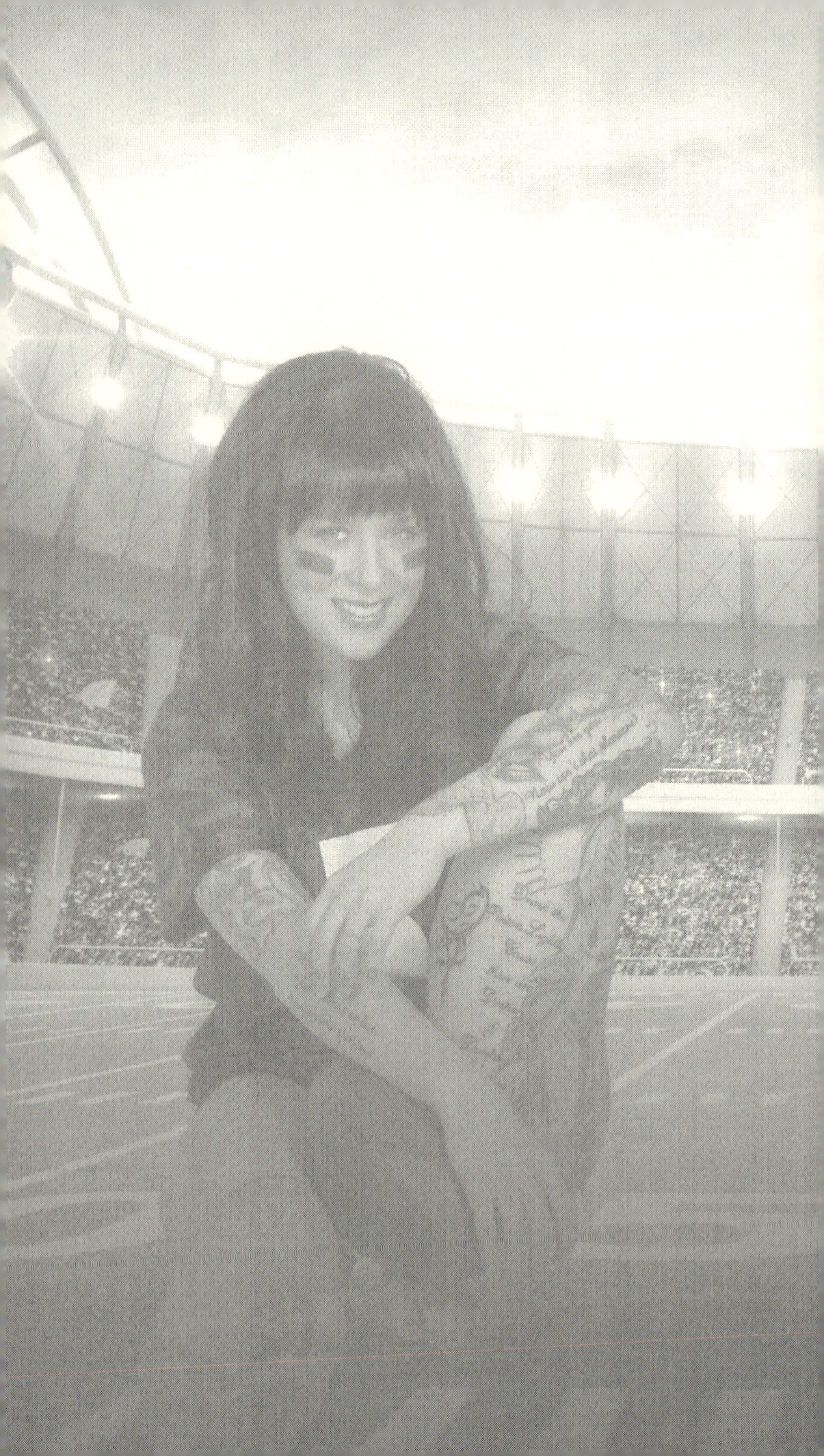

Epilogue
London

"That's it, folks. One more knee, and the Rangers have won the Championship."

Playboy, Jo-Joe, and David jump up and down with Declan's four-year-old son while the sparkling cider rains down on us. "Can you believe it, London?"

My father sits in the private box with us, chuckling as our alcohol-free suite celebrates the last and most important win of the season. "That was amazing."

I shake my head, the reality of my new world wrapping itself around me. "It's a dream come true."

Deidre, Linda, and Amelia—Declan's new fiancée—stay out of the spray, but cheer with the same enthusiasm as the guys. My soon-to-be sister-in-law throws her arms around me. "This is everything."

It's been almost six months since Deacon walked into the Overlook Hotel that fateful August evening, and now our wedding plans are set for one week from today. I've been living with Deacon for the last four months, playing

Epilogue

house and waiting for him to come home at night when we're not traveling with the team. Can I say, hotel sex in random cities... so hot! There's something about collapsing into bed after a long flight, getting a couple hours of sleep, and then being woken up by a hard cock pressed against your ass that wakes you right up.

A phone in the suite rings and Linda picks it up. "We'll be right there."

Deidre grabs mine and Amelia's hands. "Come on."

The four of us, with little Danny in tow, exit the suite, leaving the guys and my father behind. We're escorted by security guards down the elevator, through the players' tunnel, and onto the field. As soon as Deacon sees me, he holds out his hand, pulling me into his arms in front of a crowd of twenty-five thousand screaming fans. We're standing on a platform with his grandfather, father, and tonight's MVP as they award the Scott family the championship trophy.

Deacon pulls me tight against his body and puts his mouth against my ear. "This is the second best thing to happen to me this year."

"What's the first?" I have to yell to hear him over the roar of the crowd.

"Marrying the love of my life next week, of course." Deacon then kisses me so passionately that the screaming crowd fades away. Soon I see, hear, and feel nothing but him.

Daniel Jr. smacks Deacon on the shoulder, jostling us back to reality as they present Daniel Sr. with the trophy. They use this moment and platform to announce his

Epilogue

retirement as he transfers the award over to Deacon's father, the new President and CEO of the Rocky Mountain Rangers. A minute later, they pass the microphone to Deacon after he's announced as the new general manager. The entire presentation takes three minutes, and then we're standing in the background as they announce Declan as the game MVP—just as I and every other avid sports fan predicted.

The pandemonium of the crowd and the jubilation felt by the family is overwhelming, and yet, I see nothing but love smoldering in Deacon's eyes when our gazes meet. Without words, he tells me how he feels, and then, with a quirk of his lips, tells me what he wants to do to me. I give him a small raise of my eyebrow, letting him know I can't wait until we're alone later.

It's later. Deacon has me pressed against the corner of the elevator as we leave the party and head up to our suite. He has my thigh pulled up on his hip as he rubs his cock against my lace-covered pussy and kisses me with all the need we have right now. When the elevator dings, Deacon steps back and hauls me over his shoulder, fireman style.

I squeal, my bottom exposed as he walks through our suite with his big hand planted on my ass cheek. He flings me onto the bed, instantly climbing over me, his heavy body cocooning me like a weighted blanket. "I can't wait until you are Mrs. Deacon Scott."

Epilogue

Giggling, I wrap my legs around his waist. "Your team just won the championship and you're thinking about our wedding?"

"Priorities, baby." He rolls, having me straddle his waist as he runs his hands up my thighs. "I love you so much, and while I'm happy for the team and the family, I'm more focused on our future. Seeing Declan with his son, I can't wait to get you pregnant and see you round with my child."

"Why wait?" I bite my lip and grind my pussy against his erection, understanding and agreeing with his need. Ever since Declan found out he was a father and brought Amelia and Danny into our world, my maternal instincts have roared to life. Danny is an absolute doll and so much fun to play with, and Amelia is a great mom who is also quickly becoming a good friend. For the first time in my life, I feel like I'm part of something.

"Are you serious?"

A giant smile takes over my face. "I stopped taking my birth control three weeks ago. I know I should have told you, but I was ninety-nine percent sure you wouldn't mind knocking me up—sooner rather than later."

A devilish glint makes his hazel eyes sparkle as he thrusts his hips up and grips my waist. "You're going to have my baby."

Leaning forward, I kiss him softly and whisper almost in challenge. "As soon as you put one in me."

Deacon rises to every challenge I issue and has my dress up and over my head within seconds. He rolls me to my back and stands up, shedding his clothing in record

Epilogue

time. He doesn't give me time to enjoy the show, pulling me to the edge of the mattress and sliding his tongue up my inner thigh before latching onto my clit. His tongue takes me quickly to the edge while his fingers stroke my g-spot until I'm gushing my arousal. Right before I'm about to come, he thrusts his cock inside of me, sending me over the edge.

"Fuck, I love feeling you milk my cock for my seed, London."

"Deacon, please." He knows what I want. I want him to fuck me hard and mercilessly, chasing his own release. I love to feel him pounding into me, especially after I orgasm, which always makes me come a second or third time.

Within minutes he roars his release, a swell of male pride infusing the air, as if this time is different because we're purposeful in our orgasms. We collapse on the bed, a tangled heap of sweaty limbs, panting for breath.

I'm lying against his chest as he strokes my hair, his heart thumping against my cheek, thinking about my life and the unlikely scenario that brought us together. Singularly focused most of his life, Deacon never fell in love with anything other than the game. Destiny brought us together, a fake relationship his only solution to achieving his goals, and yet, not one day of our relationship felt forced. We fell into a friendship and then love effortlessly, accepting that forces greater than ourselves brought us together.

And then it hits me. "If we have a girl, what do you think of the name Destiny? Too stripperish?"

Epilogue

He chuckles. "Uh, maybe. I don't know."

"It would fit the Scott family theme. Daniel, Deacon, Declan, Deidre, Danny..."

"Maybe her middle name could be Destiny—like what brought us together."

"Exactly what I was thinking."

He smiles and closes his eyes while absently running his fingers through my hair. "I love you, London. More than I know how to put into words. More than I knew I could love another person. I'm going to spend my life making you happy. There's nothing fake about that."

"No more fake anything, handsome."

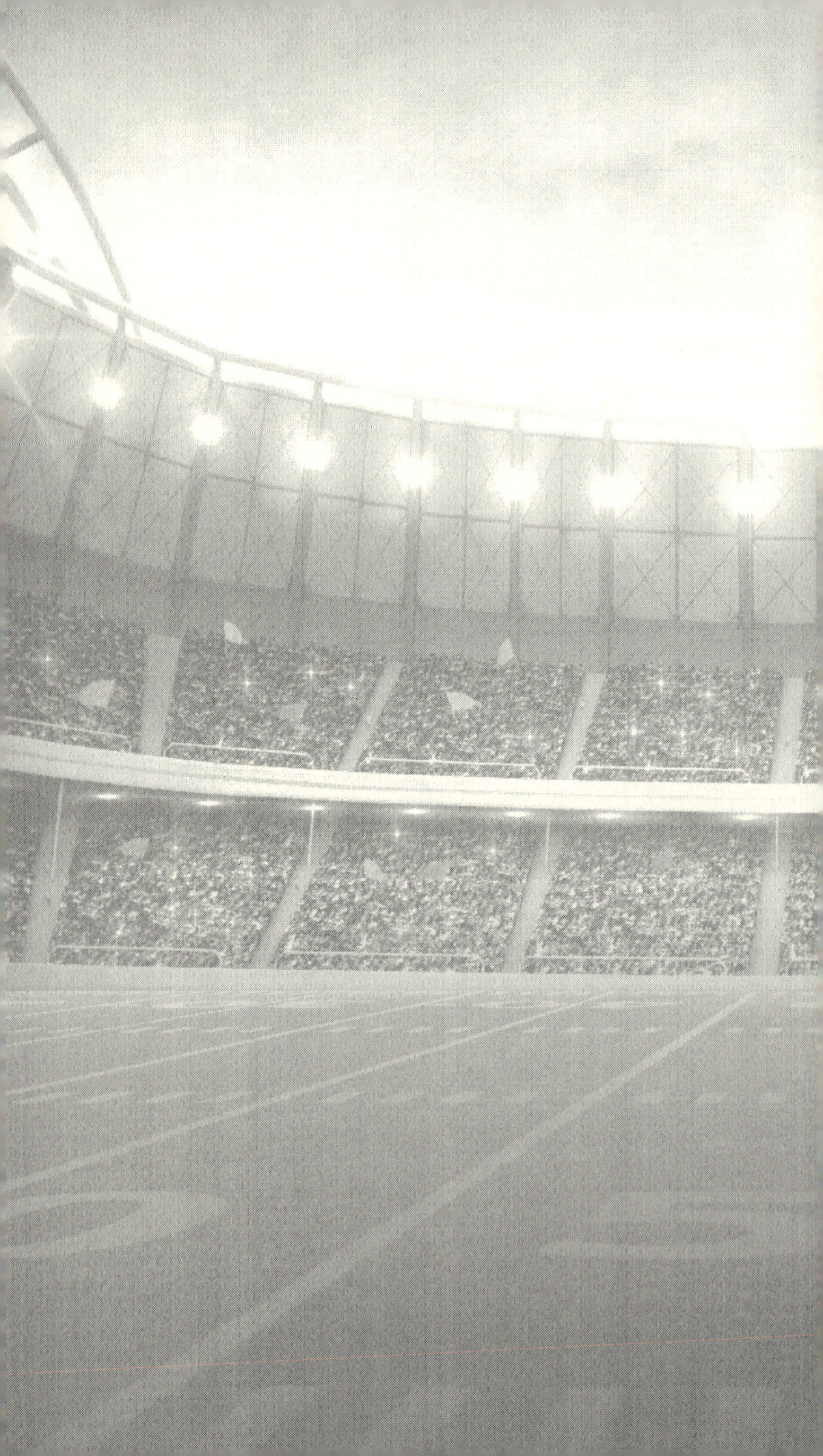

Second Epilogue
Deacon - One Week Later...

There's a knock on the door, my brother straightening my bowtie and smacking my arms at the same time my father opens it. On the other side is Robert Black, London's father.

"Sorry to interrupt, but I was hoping to have a minute alone with Deacon."

My father and brother give me a look, asking for permission to leave.

I nod, "See you guys out there."

Robert stands by with his hands clasped in front of him and waits for the door to close. "I'm sure you're aware I haven't been the best father to London, but that doesn't mean I haven't always wanted the best for her."

He presses his lips together, his eyes filling with unshed tears. "Although I couldn't give her much, I'm beyond thankful she has you now. I guess what I'm trying to say is thank you for giving my daughter the life I wasn't able to."

Second Epilogue

I offer him my hand. "I'm going to take care of her."

"Not like her old man." He shakes my hand but casts his eyes down to the carpet.

"London loves you, and I'm sure she'd like you to be around for a long time so you can be a grandfather to the children we'll have someday." I leave that veiled comment out there. The man needs to get healthy and make some way overdue changes in his life if he wants to live another twenty years.

"I'd like that. Maybe someday I'll babysit for you." He chuckles wryly.

My protective instincts flare to life and I narrow my eyes, a diatribe about how he'll never watch my children unsupervised while he's drinking teetering on the tip of my tongue—but not today. I'm not having this conversation on my wedding day. "We'll cross that bridge when it comes."

He nods. "Understood."

"Don't you need to be checking on London so you can walk your daughter down the aisle?"

"Yeah." Robert rubs the back of his neck with a shaky hand, leaving me to wonder if he's shunned alcohol so far this morning. "I guess it is that time."

Another knock at the door, and Emily the event coordinator is popping her head in without waiting for an invitation. "There you are. Father of the bride, I need you in the bridal suite."

I smile and give Robert a nod. "See you soon."

"And you." Emily points at me with her gold pen. "I need you at the front of the aisle, waiting for your bride."

Second Epilogue

"I'm all over it."

Less than ten minutes later, I'm standing with my brother at the front of a crowd of two hundred people—half of which are from the Rangers football organization. Once we made this real, I gave Mom and Deidre permission to go crazy with the wedding of the century, or at the very least, the year. Because it's mid-February in Colorado, they went with a winter theme—tree branches with icicles and twinkle lights—white, black, and Rangers red flowers with crystals and evergreens decorate the stage and aisle.

Playboy Bill, Jo-Joe, and David act as ushers, walking my mother, Deidre, and Amelia to their seats in the front.

Declan's son marches down the aisle as the ring bearer next to Rylie's daughter Nyla who took on the role as flower girl. As expected, the crowd ohhs and ahhs at the dual cuteness of the two five-year-olds.

I sneak a peek at my brother Declan, his smile a mile wide as he watches his son who practically skips down the red carpet. Old memories of a time when I was ten and Declan was four hit me, and I chuckle and whisper to my brother, "Remembering when you were a ball of barely contain energy?"

"What are you talking about? I'm still a ball of barely contain energy."

"True."

Next comes London's best friend Maryanne Merryweather wearing a silver dress with black lace overlay. Although the size of the wedding grew out of control, the bridal party remained small as designed, and even though

Second Epilogue

all my cousins are in attendance, none of them are wedding party-close to the family.

Then the music changes. *Finally, Beautiful Stranger* by Halsey plays overhead as London, with her father by her side, appears at the end of the aisle. She told me her dress would be unconventional, but the look of her takes my breath away.

"Holy shit," I mutter under my breath.

"She looks beautiful, bro," Declan whispers next to me.

"Yeah."

London is wearing a white strapless full-length gown with the gauzy material at the bottom fading into black as it approaches her feet. A black cloak with a fur-lined hood frames her face like a Disney princess, but instead of hanging from her neck, its fastened by three buttons secured under her breasts, hoisting her creamy, ample, tattooed cleavage up and drawing all my attention.

She stares at me as they approach, her purple eyes vibrant against the kohl-rimmed lashes. Her Ranger red painted lips—no doubt, Deidre's doing—are pressed together momentarily as she holds back tears.

"Hi." She smiles as her father gives me her hand.

"Hey back." I bring her fingers up to my mouth and kiss each digit.

Looking down at her dress, she quirks her eyebrow, teasing me with a smirk. "Too much?"

"You are perfect in every way and so fucking beautiful it takes my breath away."

"You look handsome, too."

Second Epilogue

The officiant starts, leading us through the basics. London and I debated writing our own vows. One, she's not a public speaking kind of woman, and two, flowery words aren't my thing. But then one night they poured out of me and I captured them, prepared to say them either in front of our friends, family, and teammates, or in private while naked in bed.

It was only two hours ago that I learned I would recite them to her now.

"I understand you have written your own vows?" the officiant asks.

I nod, taking both of London's hands in mine. Grinning down at her, I rub my thumbs over her fingers, my heart so full it's on the verge of bursting. "This has been one hell of a season, and I'm not talking about football. Without ever laying eyes on you, you intrigued my soul. And then I saw how beautiful you are and every other part of me became intrigued too." I waggle my eyebrows, and she blushes and shakes her head. "At first, I didn't want to admit it to myself because it seemed too crazy, and rushing headfirst into anything other than a defensive back isn't my style. It only took one talk with my baby brother for everything to change. *If you like her, and you want her, you might find that you love her, too. What are you waiting for?* As soon as I admitted my truth, I knew I couldn't live another day without you in my arms and by my side. I love you London, like I've never loved before, and I can't wait to build a future with you. You are my ride-or-die, and I'm yours—forevermore."

Second Epilogue

London

I wipe away the tears falling down my cheeks and suck in a shaky breath. "I can't believe I'm here right now. Not even in my wildest fantasies did I think this would happen to me. I'm not just talking about marrying you, the love of my life, but getting married in general. I was prepared to spend my life alone—me and Crow sharing leftovers in my one-bedroom apartment. You know that trust doesn't come easily to me, and yet from the moment you walked into our reunion, something told me to trust you. And I do, implicitly. I trust you to be my friend, my lover, my ride-or-die—and you can trust me to be the same, forevermore. As our friendship grew, I tried to shield my heart from you, but when I look back, I realize you won my love that first night when you chose gelato over a drink with genuine enthusiasm. That showed me what kind of guy you are deep down beneath the stunning good looks and million-dollar smile. That showed me you were the guy destined for me. I love you more than I realized I could love another person, and I'm so happy to be your wife."

We exchange rings, Danny vibrating with excitement as Declan helps him give them to us, and then the officiant is telling Deacon to kiss the bride. Deacon takes me into his arms like only he can, sliding one hand underneath my cloak, the other cupping the back of my neck, his kiss slow and deep.

"I love you, Mrs. Scott," he murmurs against my lips.

Second Epilogue

"I love you more, Mr. Scott."

The crowd hoots and hollers, bring a deep blush to my cheeks as we walk down the aisle. Emily is waiting for us at the end of the Rangers red carpet runner, but Deacon shakes his head and waves her off before she can speak. "I need a few minutes of privacy with my wife."

Emily sighs. "Yes, yes. Go to the bridal suite and have your moment, but remember you still have pictures to take, toasts to receive, and a cake to cut, so don't mess up her hair or makeup."

Deacon pulls me down the hallway toward the suite, murmuring, "I make no promises."

I giggle as he pulls me into the suite and locks the door behind him, immediately shedding his jacket and tossing it over the chair. "Fucking hell. We should have eloped like you suggested months ago."

"When I suggested that, it wasn't a proper engagement."

"At least then you wouldn't be wearing so many layers." He wraps his hands around my waist and pulls me into his body while backing me against the nearest wall. He smiles down at me and places a sweet kiss to the tip of my nose. "Exactly how many layers are underneath this dress?"

"Too many for what you're thinking. It took three motivated women to get me into this dress. There has to be twenty pounds of satin, tulle, and gauze fluffing out this dress, so it'll take more than one motivated husband to get me out and then back into it."

Deacon drops to a knee in front of me, gathering up

Second Epilogue

the hems of my skirt. "I think you underestimate your husband's determination."

Giggling, I shake my head and brace my back against the wall. "Emily's going to kill you."

"I'm pretty sure I can take her." Deacon flings my skirt over his head and slides his hands up my outer thighs and around my hips, settling my left knee on his shoulder. I hear him groan under the yards of fabric before he pushes aside my thong and slides his tongue against my swollen pussy.

I moan, leaning my head back and casting my gaze to the ornate ceiling with its decorative trim. With my dress in the way, I can do nothing but grip the chair rail and ride my husband's mouth as he expertly brings me to climax. Deacon never fails, his lips and tongue pure magic meant only for me.

Trying to keep the sex sounds down to a minimum, I bite my lip as I cry out my release. Deacon's fingers dig into my hips as he laps up the arousal gushing out of me, lifting me to my tiptoes as he eats my pussy with renewed enthusiasm. I know my man, this means one orgasm isn't going to be enough for him. I pant as a second, harder climax crashes over, my leg unable to hold up my quivering body any longer.

But as always, Deacon has me, lifting me in his arms until I once again have control over my limbs. He's kissing my thighs as he sets my shaking feet on the ground and then he slides my thong down my legs until it's wrapped around my ankles.

"What are you doing?"

Second Epilogue

He comes out from underneath my dress and lifts one foot then the other, twirling my black and white lace panty around his index finger. He wipes his mouth with the scrap of material and then stuffs it in his pocket. "These are mine now."

"You're going to walk around our wedding, greeting friends and family, with my panties in your pocket?"

"Yep." He grabs his jacket. "Are you ready to get out there?"

I reach out and grab his belt before he can step away. "Not so fast, Mr. Scott. I think we should test out my lipstick's durability."

His hazel-green eyes spark to life, and a deep growl reverberates in his chest. "Baby, you know I love your mouth. But if you start that, we'll never get out of here."

A heavy hand bangs on the door, Emily calling to us from the other side. "Okay, you two. We have a schedule to keep."

"Be right there," I yell back.

Deacon slides his coat on and then checks his face in the mirror before offering me his hand. "Come on, baby. Let's enjoy this party so we can get home and throw the actual party tonight."

I follow him out the door, Emily's eyes searching my face. "Your hair and makeup look good."

"I wasn't kissing her face," he says nonchalantly.

I blush. "Deacon!"

"What? She said not to mess up your hair or makeup, so I didn't."

Second Epilogue

Emily smiles and casts her eyes down, giggling under her breath. "You've got yourself a good man, London."

Rolling my eyes, I follow him. "Yeah, I do."

Also by Kameron Claire

The list of books by *moi* has become quite large and overwhelming to put in the back matter of each book. With over 45+ titles out in the world, it's better to direct you to my website which is constantly being updating with new information.

As far as Rangers Football series goes; there are 6 titles. Check out the Rangers Football Series ebooks / paperbacks on my website. As requested, I'll also be putting these out in Large Print.

- Play Action Fake (fake relationship / opposites attract)
- Quarterback Sneak (secret baby / second-chance)
- Personal Foul (marshmallow hero / boss babe energy)
- Two-Point Conversion (MFM / twins / girl-next-door)
- Red Zone (single dad / nanny / forbidden)
- Man Coverage (MM / Teammate / Friends-to-Lovers)

About the Author

USA Today Bestselling Author Kameron Claire writes stories with witty tongues, wicked needs, and wild deeds.

Her full length and short, steamy contemporary and paranormal romances emphasize strong female leads and the protective alpha men who know how to love and support kick-ass, take-charge women. She may not NEED him to save her, but she WANTs him to love, support, and most of all, RAVISH her.

Many of her stories contain military veterans, boss babes, gentle yet dominant men, and goofy K9 hijinks. While most of her stories are MF, she also has a hot series of reverse harem romance, as well as paranormal in development.

Find me everywhere via linktr.ee/kameronclaire

Made in the USA
Middletown, DE
21 July 2023